Critical comments about Thomas E. Kennedy's Copenhagen novels:

Praise for _DANISH FALL_, Book 4 of _The Copenhagen Quartet_

"...*Danish Fall* juggles skillfully and entertainingly with a dozen fates whose Danish dream threatens to end as a nightmare...juggles so it stings with suspense...at once a beautiful and tragic portrait of the capital and its soul."
　　—Tonny Vorm, *Information* (Copenhagen)

"...very sensitive, musical and melancholy stroll out into the Queen's state... spiced with Kennedy's Celtic humor... Kennedy's force is his ear for good dialogue, those understated conversations between irony and intimacy of which Anglo-Saxon and Irish literature have always been world champion..."
　　—Bo Tao Michaelis, *Politiken* (Copenhagen)

"Kennedy writes of the lower points of life, of demotion and dismissal, of divorce and disappointment, but writes with a sardonic humor that relieves the mood and allows the reader to engage with the characters, both young and old. The final novel in the Quartet maintains both the standards and the attractions of the three earlier novels on life in Copenhagen."
　　—*Bookview Ireland* "Book of the Week"

"...owes much to Nabokov, Joyce, and Dylan Thomas while confirming Kennedy's reputation as a master of English prose... a whirlwind of intense, rich language and a poetic vision of the things that really matter in a man's life."
　　—Linda Lappin, *South Carolina Review*

"...has lost none of the steam and exubernce of the previous three and this might be the best. Few writers deliver the goods with such consistency..."
　　—*Cape Cod Voice* "Favorite Books From 2005"

"*Danish Fall* offers further proof of Kennedy's exquisite mastery of the writing craft...a beautifully sculpted novel...yet another Kennedy masterpiece."
　　—Liam Jennings, *Irish Edition* (Philadelphia)

Praise for _GREENE'S SUMMER_, Book 3 of *The Copenhagen Quartet*

"...wise and astonishingly beautiful... Despite its unflinching look at humanity's greatest horrors, this masterful novel eventually passes beyond terror, and the reader is left contemplating the healing powers of kind daughters, ministering angels and the sad beauty of Danish summer."
*- Kansas City Star*

"...powerful sprinkles of flashback and review which evoke the unreal nightmare of torture... A Consummate exploration of the themes of violence, religion in modern Europe, the rise of antisocial tendencies in the great social democracies, and love... (*Greene's Summer)* lacks nothing... Kennedy is a master craftsman..."
*- Books Ireland*

"In a masterfully constructed narrative, Kennedy leads the reader through the lives of (the characters) and intertwines them into an utterly compelling tale.... he reveals the unspoken words and desires, the fierce determination of the human heart, and the possibility of healing."
*- BookView Ireland*

"Destinies meet at one another's crossroads in the third part of this American, Danish-resident author's moody noir quartet about Copenhagen... Kennedy is well on his way to placing the Danish capital city on the international literary map..."
*-Five star review in Euroman*

"...an elegy to the human heart...a glorious novel by a modern master."
*-Irish Edition*

"(Kennedy) has populated his fictional Copenhagen with American daydreamers, Russian prostitutes, and Arabian Muslims... *Greene's Summer* unfolds as a love triangle between Bernardo Greene, a Chilean torture victim being treated in Copenhagen, Michela Ibsen who has come out of a violent marriage, and her new lover Voss Andersen who is caught in his own sexual obsession. On Copenhagen's streets...Bernardo and Michela bump into one another and attempt to find out if they dare fall in love."
*- Information* (Copenhagen)

"Tragic, wise, comic, profound, *Greene's Summer* is an epic of the human heart struggling for meaning and redemption."
*- The Literary Review*

"An exiled Chilean saved by angels is the main character of successful best-seller...a chain of dramatic incidents through the course of one summer..."
　　　　　　　　　　—*Las Ultimas Noticias* (Santiago, Chile)

"With generous and elegant prose, Thomas Kennedy takes us from the darkest, most violent regions of our collective behavior to our most exalted: our enduring hope for something higher, our need to forgive and be forgiven, our human hunger to love and be loved. *Greene's Summer* is a deeply stirring novel suffused with intelligence, grace , and that rarest of qualities – written or otherwise – wisdom."
　　　　　　　　　　—Andre Dubus III, author of *House of Sand and Fog*

Praise for *BLUETT'S BLUE HOURS*, Book 2 of *The Copenhagen Quartet*

"No one writes about the loves and lives of men better than Kennedy, including their relationships with their own children."
　　　　　　　　　　—John Mark Eberhart, *Kansas City Star,* "Noteworthy Books of 2003"

"...like blues from a saxophone, yes, in jazz style and blue tone, comparable with Dan Turrell's Copenhagen crime books with murder in the dark and much more..."
　　　　　　　　　　—Bo Tao Michaëlis, *Politiken* (Copenhagen)

"...Kennedy's second part of a planned noir quartet about Copenhagen is a moody and charming acquaintance..."
　　　　　　　　　　—Tonny Vorm, *Information* (Copenhagen)

"...names like Paul Auster as well as Dan Turrell floated into my consciousness while I read...a journey through the less smiling sectors of Copenhagen and its nightlife..."
　　　　　　　　　　—Ulrich Wolf, *Østerbro Avis* (Copenhagen)

"...all the accouterments you'd expect from this inventive author – unflinching characterizations, a wildly inventive plot, and the taste of jazz and booze on every page. Kennedy is a writer's writer and a reader's fortunate discovery."
　　　　　　　　　　—Michael Lee, *Cape Cod Voice* ("Our Favorite Books, 2003")

"...a great novel!"　—*Irish Voice*

"...A beautifully sculpted novel, *Bluett's Blue Hours* showcases Kennedy's peculiar genius for physical and emotional description."
　　　　　　　　　　—*Irish Edition*

Praise for *KERRIGAN'S COPENHAGEN*, Book 1 of *The Copenhagen Quartet*

"Here is Copenhagen...conscious and sensual...a Cathedral of the night with fantastic chapels of cafés and restaurants...and women...a loving hymn to Copenhagen...everything is more beautiful written in English ink from an Irish-American fountain pen."
    —Boa Tao Michaëlis, *Politiken*

"...a can-opener to Danish cultural life...the more Kerrigan learns about Copenhagen the happier he gets..."
    —Danish Television DR 2 "Bestseller"

"...a declaration of love to Copenhagen..."    —Danish Television "Lorry"

"This must be the first time that The King's Copenhagen to this extent has been both scene and stuff for such a comprehensive novel..."
    —Niels Barfoed, *Politiken*

"...a blockbuster...a declaration of love to jazz and Copenhagen...a classic love story..."
    —Frederiksberg Radio

"Kennedy has placed Copenhagen on a level with Joyce's Dublin."
    — David Applefield, *Frank* (Paris)

"...an exciting journey for the reader, a wonderful, delightful read...a remarkable achievement...an excellent companion for a visit to Copenhagen."
    —*Books Ireland*

"...a wildly inventive novel, simultaneously tender, raunchy, intelligent and uproariously funny..."
    —*Cape Cod Voice* ("Our Favorite Fiction 2002")

"... sumptuous and rich, sensuous and intelligent, witty and joyous, like Copenhagen itself, the living heart of this wonderful novel..."
    —Linda Lappin, *The Literary Review*

"...Kennedy's power to relate sight and sound on the page borders on the supernatural – becomes even more resonant amplified by the Copenhagen experiences of Ben Webster, Stan Getz, and Chet Baker..."
    —*Abiko* (Tokyo)

THOMAS E. KENNEDY

# a passion in the desert

AUTHOR OF THE COPENHAGEN QUARTET

2007

# A PASSION IN THE DESERT

# ACKNOWLEDGMENTS

The lines quoted on pages 21 and 95 are from Matthew Arnold's "Dover Beach." The lines quoted in Chapter 8 are from the film *Taxi Driver*, written by Paul Schrader. The lines quoted from "Band of Gold" were written by Jack Taylor and Bob Musel. The lines quoted from "Good Luck Charm" are by Aaron Schroeder and Wally Gold. Italicized lines on page 22 are from Pablo Neruda's "Poetry" and James Joyce's *Ulysses*. The quatrain on page 25 is by Emily Dickinson. Lines quoted on pages 26 and 39 from Counting Crows are by Adam Duritz. The Led Zeppelin lines on page 28 are from "Black Dog" by Jimmy Page, Robert Plant, and John Paul Jones. Some of the italicized lines in the "Shadow King" sections are quoted or adapted from the writings of Aleister Crowley. Page 52 and Chapter Seven include lines quoted from the Jim Morrison/Doors songs, "Love Me Two Times, Babe," "Hello, I love You," and "The End." The lines quoted on page 61 are from T. S. Eliot's *Four Quartets*. The line quoted on page 93 is from "Baby It's You" by David/Bacharach/Williams. The lines on page 161 are from A. E. Housman's "Loveliest of Trees," and the line quoted from the song "Jenny Jenny Jenny" is by Little Richard Penniman.

ISBN: 1-877655-52-X
978-1-877655-52-4
Library of Congress Number: 2006938962

First Edition: April 2007

Wordcraft of Oregon, LLC
David Memmott, Editor
P.O. Box 3235
La Grande, OR 97850
www.wordcraftoforegon.com

Cover Design: Kristin Johnson, redbat design
Cover art: Andi Olsen,   www.andiolsen.com
Author photo: Alice Maud Guldbrandsen

Printed in the USA by McNaughton & Gunn

for Daniel and Isabel
and always, for Alice

## BOOKS BY THOMAS E. KENNEDY:

Novels
   A Passion in the Desert (2007)
   Danish Fall (2005)
   Greene's Summer (2004)
   Bluett's Blue Hours (2003)
   Kerrigan's Copenhagen, A Love Story (2002)
   The Book of Angels (1997)
   A Weather of the Eye (1996)
   Crossing Borders (1990)

Story Collections
   Cast Upon the Day (2007)
   Drive Dive Dance & Fight (1997)
   Unreal City (1996)

Essay Collections
   The Literary Traveler (2005)*
   Realism & Other Illusions: Essays on the Craft of Fiction (2002)

Literary Criticism
   American Short Story Award Series (1993)
   Robert Coover: A Study of the Short Fiction (1992)
   The American Short Story Today (1991)**
   Andre Dubus: A Study of the Short Fiction (1988)

Anthologies
   (special anthology issues of The Literary Review or
      Review of ContemporaryFiction)
   The Secret Lives of Writers (2001)*
   Poems & Sources (2000)
   Stories & Sources (1998)
   Small Gifts of Knowing: New Irish Writing (1997)
   New Danish Fiction (1995)***

*with Walter Cummins
**with Henrik Specht
***with Frank Hugus

www.thomas-e-kennedy.com
www.thecopenhagenquartet.com

"Do as thou wilt shall be the whole of the law."
-Aleister Crowley

"In the desert you see there is everything and nothing…. It is God without mankind."
-Honoré de Balzac

# Chapter One

Somewhere over the state line, Twomey wakes in his berth in the dark and realizes the train has stalled. He wonders where they are—how far into Vermont?—feels the cold through his covers, reaches up to his right and touches the freezing window glass. There are voices in the corridor outside the door of his compartment.

A woman is speaking. "It's from the cold sometimes," she says. "There are gaps in the electric current. You hit a gap and the train stops. They have to move the gap."

It occurs to Twomey that what she says is nonsense. There is an edge to her voice. Near hysteria. *Lucky I'm in bed. Best place to be for something like this.* He presses the illuminator on his watch: three a.m. The train is due in to Montpelier at six. Or *was*. How long have they been stalled here? No way to know. The woman's voice is moving away along the corridor. He hears the murmur of a man's voice, low, words indistinct. Do they have light out there. Flashlight maybe. Or cigarette lighter. If you still smoked you'd have a lighter handy now to light your way here. Ironic.

In the quiet he becomes aware that there is no sound at all coming from the train. It seems to him they usually vibrate, or hum a little at least. Don't usually go completely dead like this. Unsettling. He thinks for a moment of calling Jenny at home on Long Island to let her know, then that he can't call her at this hour, even if he had a cell phone. He doesn't believe in cell phones. Another irony.

The thought of Jenny reminds him of what happened when he got home from school yesterday. As he packed his bag, Jenny looked into the room and asked, "Who's the joker?" Her face strange. "Come and see," she said, and he followed her into her workroom, saw the baby doll in the cage she'd been working on, a steak knife clutched into one of its little latex hands.

"New detail?" he asked.

"Yeah, but the question is who did it?"

"You mean you didn't put the knife there?"

"That's right."

Twomey studied the doll, the red eyes, open mouth, teeth. The arm holding the steak knife was bent upward, overhand grip, so it appeared about to stab. *Where Are the Children?* He remembered he wanted to ask her was she reading that, but this was not the moment to ask. "Who could have done it?" he asked. "Maybe Larry goofing around."

She shook her head. "I already asked him."

Funny, he thought, that neither of them suggested Jimbo. Maybe she just automatically ruled him out. "Where's Jimbo?" he asked.

"Gone to stay with one of his friends for the weekend."

"Which friend?"

"A classmate. Tony something up in Scarsdale. He left a phone number."

"Well if it wasn't Larry, it must have been Jimbo. There are only four of us here. I didn't do it, so if you didn't and Larry didn't, it could only be Jimbo." She didn't agree. But they found no explanation. Later, without mentioning it to her, Twomey found the phone number Jimbo had left, scrawled in pencil on a scrap of looseleaf paper. He closed himself into his study with the cordless and dialed. A man's voice answered, quiet, ungiving. Twomey explained who he was, asked to speak to Jimbo.

"There's no Jimbo here." Flat.

"He's supposed to be staying with Tony."

"Well, he ain't here, mister, and there's no Tony either."

He repeated the number to see if he dialed incorrectly.

"That's the number, but there's no one named Jimbo or Tony here, buddy."

"May I ask who I've phoned to?"

"No. Now don't call here again."

Twomey sat staring at the number pencilled on a scrap of paper, scrawled. That '5' could be an '8', that '3' could be a '5'. He thought of trying again, each possibility, but stuck the paper back beneath the edge of the phone and returned to Jenny's studio. She had taken the knife out of the doll's hand and laid it alongside the cage. The look of it there made Twomey uneasy. The thought of all the knives in a kitchen, any intruder could arm himself to the teeth. Filet you in your sleep.

The tip of his nose is cold. He massages it, realizes his fingers and toes are cold, too. Sometimes down way below zero up here. Could freeze to death in the train. He pictures the snow outside, the landscape, silvery dark and quiet. The sky with white dark clouds. Pictures himself walking the rest of the way, boots crunching in the snow. Get lost, tired, sit down to rest and your eyes droop, you sleep, never found again. Like Jack London's "To Build a Fire." One of the first stories you ever read, way back when? In some schoolbook reader. Childhood. Winter. All those snowmen, snowball fights.

He remembers when he was waiting for the flat on his bike to be patched the other day—another goddamn flat, three kids came along the street on their way home from school, two boys and a girl. He watched from behind the window of the bike shop. The boys were having a snowball fight, dipping to pack snow between their mittens, pelting each other, laughing, shouting. The little girl was maybe two years younger than them, eight maybe. She watched from the side for a while, then finally stooped and made a snowball. Twomey watched to see which of the boys she would throw for, but she turned away and threw the snowball at a stop sign. She missed. It flew past and disappeared in a snowbank and she stood there looking after it. Saddened Twomey.

Never had a daughter, he thinks now, but then remembers what he does not wish to think about, could have been a girl. If at all. Most likely not at all. No. Katey's daughter. No.

His mouth is dry. The sink is just below the edge of his berth, and he wonders if he could manage to get some water from the bottle beneath it, pictures himself fumbling it, spilling water in the cold

15

compartment, wet feet, maybe get his shoes, too. No good. There was a bottle of Hennessey in his shoulder bag, but that would just make him more thirsty. Take it for the cold. But they say it makes you lose warmth actually.

He closes his eyes, realizes there is no difference between staring into the dark or closing his eyes. Only that your eyeballs begin to get cold. If there was light in here, he thinks, I could see my breath I bet. He pulls the cover up closer to his chin, slips his hands down between his thighs, thinks about that, maybe put himself to sleep.

A loud, distinct snap sounds in the dark. Twomey catches his breath. It was close by. In here? He half sits up, on his hip, back to the window, right fist balled, listens.

Nothing.

The air is moving. He feels it. Cold air moving across his cheek. He can hear the faint whistle of breath in his own nostril, feels sweat on his forehead, his back. He moves very slowly, quietly into a better position. Better for what? In case someone is here, about to jump him. Or stealing his things. He listens for any movement. Get out of bed, he thinks. Let them know you're here, awake. They might think you're asleep, come in to rip you off. Who's they?

"Who's there?" he demands suddenly. "You're in the wrong compartment." No nonsense tone. Let them know it's a man. There is no answer, no sound, only the seep of cold air on his face. He feels he could sleep now, if he lay his head down, but that would be sick. He remembers the two drinks he had in the bar car before going to bed last night, and the tuna salad sandwich that he thought he might barf up for a while there. Bad dream maybe. More of gravy than the grave in you.

His heart lurches as that loud snap sounds out again in the dark, and he hops up onto his knees on the berth, both fists balled, eyes desperately searching in the dark, even as he observes himself, sees a comic element to it—a grown man flailing about in the dark, remembers how when he was a kid, fifteen, sixteen, he was often terrified in the dark, convinced that if he opened his eyes there might be a face right in front of his, fears he hasn't felt or even thought about in years.

He notices that the air is still again, no longer moving on his face. Compartment door, he thinks. Was open, now it's shut again. That snap, the lock popping. Someone with a credit card or something?

The train motor begins to idle again. After many moments, he swings his legs out from beneath the covers, drops to the floor, swings his arms. The space is empty. He feels along the wall the whole way around, feels for the wall switch. Light fills the little compartment. The door is shut, but it swings open when he tries the catch. He was sure he'd locked that before he went to sleep. Never forget a thing like that.

The train vibrates comfortingly. He flips the lock switch on the compartment door, tests to make sure it is locked, flicks off the light and swings back up beneath the covers. The train begins to roll, and Twomey feels himself drifting. He snaps awake, recognizes how pleasant sleep is, fades off again.

In the dream he is outside his house, walking around and around the outside of the house, looking in. He hears a strange voice and keeps looking, peering in through windows and the glass on doors, down into the basement, the upstairs windows. He sees people there, looks closer, but it is only the boys, his wife, no one else, except there is still this voice, this strange voice that he cannot place.

# Chapter Two

Montpelier is filled with writers. Across the snowbound campus at the top of the steep hill, writers in winter garb, brightly colored ski-suits, anoraks, army field jackets with fleece-lined hoods, walk to and fro from building to building, to attend lectures, buy coffee, browse in the little bookshop. Twomey knows Montpee and has promised Jeff Burns a tour of the local bars after the last session today. He has already delivered his own talk and gave his reading, both of which went well, and all he really wants to do now is have fun.

He sits in one of many folding chairs in Nobel Lounge, listening to a lecture on "Hamlet as a Moral Metaphor for our Times," while Burns, beside him, grumbles, "That word, moral, should be seen and not heard."

At the lectern, standing before a dusty portrait of Charles Nobel, founder of something or other, an associate professor from Arkansas is quoting William Meister on *Hamlet*. "'The effects of a great action laid upon a soul unfit for the performance of it.'"

"That is a very rusty concept," Twomey whispers to Burns. "A soul unfit to perform?"

"You watch," Burns says. "This will all lead to some PC brownie points."

"Hey I got an idea. We're not far from the door. Let's split."

"That's a plan."

"Now?" Twomey whispers.

"Now."

With self-effacing smiles and shrugs of apology, they tiptoe to the door while the lecturer makes some point about cultural multiplicity.

Out in the cold bright air, they trudge across the campus green, white now with snow, toward the hill down into town. "I don't know about you but I do not intend to eat in the cafeteria tonight," Twomey says.

"No way."

"You want some Mexican?"

"You bet."

At the far edge of the campus, a green depot mailbox is graffiti'd with the words *YOU KNOW WHAT YOU'VE DONE!* in black spray paint. Twomey wants to write it down in his notebook, decides he doesn't want to take off his gloves and dig inside his jacket. "Must be minus fifteen," he says.

"We should have skis for this descent," Burns says. The hill is steep and slippery. Sunlight glints harshly off patches of ice.

"Any of your students here?" Burns asks.

"Seen two so far. Know them? Green and Serafino."

"Surf City. The Beach Boy. Looks straight out of Southern Cal."

"Right."

"Who's the other one?"

"Green. Older kid. Little kind of weird, I think."

"Intense dark-haired guy? Mid-twenties."

"Right."

"He's weird. I saw him in the cafeteria once just staring at me. No matter what I did, where I put my eyes, turned my head away, glance back and he's staring at me, still in the exact same position, his fork in the air, poised over his lunch. Figured I could back him off with direct response, you know? So I stared right back at him, but he kept right on staring at me, blank-faced, just staring. Pissed me off. Spooked me, too. I hear he was in the Gulf War. Wonder was he ever in Oklahoma."

"Hey, don't knock Oklahoma—fine litmag comes out of there. *Cimarron Review*."

"Right. Good mag. If only they'd proofread."

"Picky picky."

It is work descending the hill. Burns begins to huff between his

20

words. "Hey, you see that woman over there? Coming up the hill on the other side?"

A short woman in a red anorak, black curls showing as a fringe from beneath her hood, is moving slowly up the hill, looking all around her with a liberal smile.

"She's a poet. Asked me would I blurb her last collection. So I read the thing and it's like *okay*, nothing great, but good enough that I can hype up something for the jacket. I write a blurb that is maybe a little more than ethically defensible, but what the hell, are we here to help or hinder? I send it to her, figure she'll be happy, figure, who knows? She might even desire my bod in gratitude. She sends me a letter complaining that the blurb failed to focus on the two strongest poems in the book, asking how could I have missed that and if I don't want to reconsider what I've written in light of that."

"What'd you do?"

"Didn't answer. Brassy bitch," he says as the woman waves, and he smiles, returning the wave in a motion that looks like he's wiping a window.

"You're a bit of a hypocrite, aren't you?" says Twomey.

"Yes."

"I thought so. Me, too. Watch out, let's cross, here comes Tony Oneyed, he's after me to set up a reading for him, come on."

"He's after *everyone* to set up a reading for him. Everyone is after everyone to set up a reading for them. Hey, by the way, could you set up a reading for me?"

"Not on your life."

"Well, fuck you, then, dickhead. See if I set one up for you."

"Hey, I'm sorry, I didn't mean it."

"Too late, buddy. You blew it. Unless you offer me a reading."

"Paid?"

"Let me think about that."

"Let *me* think about *that*, then."

They hike diagonally across the road, circling behind the tail of a Chevy pick-up moving carefully up the slippery incline.

At the base of the hill is another blue metal depot mailbox, this one sporting the words, *YOU DON'T DESERVE A FUTURE AND*

*THE FUTURE DOESN'T DESERVE YOU.*

"Hey," Burns says, "They got some pretty weird graffiti here for a quaint little New England town."

"Capital city, boy."

"Yeah, population ten thousand two hundred six."

"Five. I heard Charles Newburg moved south yesterday. To become a writer."

"How about some strong drink, Burns?"

"Hey, you're a goddamn alcoholic, aren't you?"

"Know the definition of an alcoholic?"

"I'll bite."

"Someone who drinks more than his doctor."

Twomey knows Montpelier from a workshop he taught here a couple of summers. "Okay," he says, "Here's the selection. Across the road here we got Charlie-O's, your local redneck dive. They boast a national award-winning Charlie-O logo tee shirt that you can buy for eight bucks. They also have, in the way of food, a giant screw-top jar of ancient, pickled, boiled eggs, without shells, and another one with blood sausages. The beer is good, there are pool tables, and sometimes there are fights. And don't get fresh with the barmaid. Her husband's president of the local Hells Angels. Down the street to your right there is The Thrush, quaint little sidestreet joint with good beer, good sandwiches, agreeable atmosphere, and twofers at blue hour. You can also get a snack, plate of fried mushrooms, for example. Delish. Further down on the other side is a hotel bar whose name escapes me. Very roomy place with spiffy waitresses, though the beer is sometimes flat and the food is sporadic. To the left and further up, we have Julio's, the Mex restaurant. Decent food and beer, but do not drink the gin. Other than that, several blocks up is a decent beef house, and about two miles further up there is one Blue Fedora Motel which is frequented by people with illicit liaisons to maintain. Good restaurant."

"You know that place?"

"Only as a witness."

"I bet. I wouldn't mind one of them illicit liaisons right about now myself. Anyplace else?"

"I've been through the catalogue now."

"One question. Do they understand the word *martini*?"

"Is that how it's going to be today?"

"The Blue Hour is upon us, chum. I suggest we start with one of those ancient boiled eggs and a martin, work our way forward to the Peacock…"

"That's Thrush."

"…Thrush, then, and a martin, hit the hotel bar with the spiffy waitresses see what kind of martin they serve, then, unless some spiffy waitress wants us to stay, we hook back to the boiled-egg place for one more, and by then, I would guess, we should be ready for a nice Mexican plate with a touch of claret."

"Writers are all drunkards."

"You bet. Irish birth control. Enflames the spirit, stuns the flesh. In a sense," Burns says, "this getting drunk now could be viewed as a moral act, to render us incapable of succumbing to the only too human temptations of the flesh."

"A great action laid upon a soul unfit to perform it.

"You horny cuss."

"Actually I'm not horny, just thirsty."

"A honeymoon of the hand."

"Every man his own wife."

"Try the left for strange stuff."

By the time they run the entire circuit of the town back to Julio's, Twomey forgets his own advice not to drink the gin there and orders another martini. Julio's is on the second floor and they sit at tables by the window where they have a view one way down to the street, the other into the bar. Twomey is trying hard not to get wrecked, but Burns, who is at least two drinks up on him, makes it look like such fun he has difficulty monitoring his sips from the beautiful inverted glass bell of the cocktail glass. Burns has a manner of drinking that makes Twomey think of William Powell in *The Thin Man*. You can almost taste it just watching him.

"Oh oh," Burns says, "Don't look now but look at the table over beside the potted palm there. Do you know that woman? Young adjunct from the department. Whatserface, Janet. Janet Fallow."

"*Fallow*? That's not a name, it's an adjective." Twomey glances back—discreetly he thought—but just as he does the young woman waves and flashes a smile. He smiles, waves, says, "She's looking at us."

"I don't think so," says Burns. "She's lookin' at me."

"I remember her now."

"I bet you do. She is gorgeous."

"Hey hey," says Twomey. "Decorum. Control. We're too old for that kind of stuff."

"Hey, Twom, use it or lose it."

"Honeymoon of the hand, remember?"

A laugh tripped over Burns's lips. "Being afraid to marry on earth/They masturbated all they were worth. Hey, Twom, I need some strange stuff. And Ms. Fallow is, how you say? Very *kallipyge*. And sweet-*kteised*."

Twomey glances across the table at his colleague's moustached face in the shadowy light of the bar, wondering if this is all talk and show. He tries to fit this Burns together with the Burns he and Jenny have entertained with wife for dinner, the couple who are aching to have children. It doesn't fit. But what ever does? He wishes they could keep things light and easy here, but finds himself asking, "Hey, are you serious?"

Burns gives him a William Powell lift of the eyebrow, enquiring. "Serious?"

"You really out to get laid here?"

Burns's smile is not cryptic.

"What about Susan?" The question sounds priggish in his own ears, but he is not sorry he asked. He sees the William Powell mask slipping away as Burns sobers to handle the question. "What *about* Susan?"

"Wouldn't you feel like, well, a *cheat*, when you got home if you, you know, well, *cheated* on her?"

"Cheated? Hey, in all honesty, I think a person shouldn't cheat himself of life. Look, nothing is simple, but I think it would be wrong not to go with your desire for a woman like that. I mean if she shares the feeling."

"So you, you're no stranger to this sort of thing?"

Burns sips his martini, turns his eyes across to Twomey in the shadowy light. "Hey, ask no questions, Fred."

"Really. Tell me. How can you fit it all together in your life? Does Susan know? Do you tell her?"

"I think she does. In some way she probably does. But she won't ask."

"She won't?"

Burns' head shakes slowly.

"And it doesn't haunt you? You don't suffer guilt?"

"Not really, no." He fingers the stem of his glass, pops some peanuts into his mouth. "I mean, yes, a little maybe, but what's the alternative? To be haunted by *not* doing it? What's worse? Whether you marry or not you will regret it. What are we going to regret more when we're old? The things we do or the things we don't do?"

What Twomey is thinking he doesn't want to say for fear of sounding pretentious and self-aggrandizing, but Burns's words have created an image in his gin-blurred brain of human beings on some great plain like a herd of wildebeest coupling indiscriminately by turns with first one then another then another, and what he wants to say, what he is thinking is, *what about not doing a few things in order to make room for some faithfulness to a single person you love? To devote yourself to some one person because...* His eyes rise to Burns again as he realizes what he wishes to say. "Love, let us be true/To one another for the world..."

"So various, so beautiful," says Burns, and Twomey continues, "Hath really neither joy, nor love, nor light,/Nor certitude, nor peace,/Nor help for pain..."

Burns lifts his glass. "Poor Twomey. No joy, no love, no light... Come awn, man. The moving finger writes and having writ moves on and faith tis pleasant til tis past/The mischief is it will not last." He swallows the rest of his martini and is on his feet, swaying across the shadowy room like a dancer beneath the sea, moving toward Janet Fallow, and Twomey feels embarrassed for him, wants to call him back, remind him of something that might make him recognize the

25

futility of what he is trying to do, although in truth he recognizes that he only knows what he himself wants and does not want to do and cannot be certain whether it is true choice or some measure of compulsion founded in things taught him by squelched Victorian nuns or a true desire to find dignity or just a grab in the dark for something that is not there.

On the juke box Elvis Presley sings "Good Luck Charm." To have. To hold. To night. Burns is standing over Janet Fallow's table. He bows. Her smile is bright as the candle flame burning in the little glass snowball before her. Twomey's eyes drop to the glass snowball in the center of his own table. There is no candle in it. He looks at the olive-greasy remainder of martini in his stem glass. Half full. Half empty. He goes to the bar for a club soda to freshen his mouth.

Outside the light is gone. His eyes meet the cold white snow in evening dark, touching off words in his brain. He feels in his pocket for his notepad and pencil, thinks, *Give it a rest for Christ's sake, relax*, but takes out the pad, slips off his glove, writes, *His eyes meet the cold, white snow in evening dark*, stands there shivering as the dark air seeps in beneath the cuffs of his field jacket and pantlegs. He thinks of Burns upstairs with Janet Fallow, thinking of her blond face, brown eyes the color of nougat, her mouth.

The avenue is broad and Christmas glitzy, spanned with plastic fir and lights. The shop windows he passes are adorned with sprigs of colored fir, tinsel, tiny trees, elves. He stops at the illuminated window of the Bear Pond Bookshop, decorated for Christmas with a display of beatnik revivals. The faces of young Kerouac, Ginsburg, Clellon Holmes, Burroughs, Neal Cassady, Ferlinghetti. Twomey remembers how Kerouac ignited him in the sixties, remembers —when? sixty-seven?—reading *Maggie Cassady* by flashlight in a sleeping bag by the Big Sur River where he'd hitchhiked after dropping out of college. Those lost years. The desert. Katey. His eyes linger on the cover of a book titled *Rue Git le Coeur*. Street where the heart lies dead. Heart Lies Dead Street. Dead Heart Street. Heartbreak Street.

To have. To hold. To-night.

He crosses beneath the Christmas decorations, past the graffitied mailbox, **You don't deserve a future and The Future doesn't deserve you.** The words catch at his thoughts of the past, those hopeful Kerouac years, and how they spiralled out in the sixties. The desert. Katey.

A wind is rising. The Christmas festoons squeak and flop against their moorings as he begins to climb the hill. How strange to be here now in Vermont winter cold, moonlight in the snow and thinking back in time to the yellow desert. Zabriskie Point. Furnace Creek. Those years with Katey. *I am not a good person. I had no choice. No.*

She picked him out where he sat in the library in Sante Fe. *Why me? 'Cause I liked your face. Cause you were reading Neruda.*

*"Something started in my soul,"* he whispers now, seeing his breath pant white in the dark. *"Fever or forgotten wings, and I made my own way deciphering that fire."* Dead breaths I living breathe, tread dead dust.

It has begun to snow. Big soft flakes fall in the angle of the wind, a screen of diagonals on Dead Heart Street, you stupid stupid man, your life is a disgrace. You are not good.

A pick-up truck slows, passing him, and he sees the driver's bearded face watching him from the dark cab, another face, indistinct, beside him.

"Want a ride?"

"No, thanks."

"Good, cause you ain't gonna get one." The truck speeds up, fish-tails round an uphill curve. Townies. Who lives in these houses along the road? New England wood. Nice phrase. Write it down. Write it all down. Sounds better. Easier than life. This cold hill in words on a page read on a warm night in bed, cozy toes beneath the cozy covers. Words on a page easier than life, sense of control. Ennobling, too, makes it seem more noble. Or captured, no longer dangerous, like a moose head on a wall, butterfly on a pin. Dead. Yet seems alive and good. What about that bearded driver? Shadowed face in the dark cab of the truck. Put him in a book. Whose face beside him? Just a suggestion of a face. Gone now, where? Meet him in an alley and what? Nasty shit, hoped I'd accept his offer so he could peel out on me. Give him a sense of power. Or did he want to pick me up, maybe drop me off in the woods, see if he could rob me, worse? *Deliverance.* Hint of death there. Face in the shadows, slows for a look.

The hill steepens sharply toward the top. Twomey leans into the slope, face tucked down from the bite of the snow. Like tiny evil mouths nipping at his face. Mustn't be thin-skinned. Writers, of course, all are thin-skinned. Have to be. Have to be willing to hurt, consider your pain, bleed and study the blood, find words to describe the hurt.

Write some of this down or you'll forget it. Like the scrap of paper you found in your wallet in the bar when you paid for your drinks before, scribbled with *lind tree sound of the wind seeping through the leaves* and suddenly that note reminded you of the day you and your wife were out to visit her art professor last summer seated with glasses of white wine beneath a lind tree and the sound of the wind he realized was a "seeping" sound, *le mot juste*, so he excused himself to take a pee and wrote that note, stuffed it in his wallet and promptly forgot the note, the experience, the day, find it again now, half a year later, scribbled words on the torn margin of a newspaper, and it all comes back to you, even the taste of the wine, all because you found the right verb, *seep*, a whole experience encoded in ten words or less.

His left foot, he realizes, is numb from cold. His face is, too. It is cold enough for frost bite. He will have to examine his face in the mirror when he gets back inside—look for white spots. Or is it black spots? You could die here if you fell, hit your head, freeze to death. He thinks again of the bearded face in the dark cab of the truck, sees black eyes glittering at him. Did he, in fact, *see* black eyes glittering or is that a detail added for effect? How could he ever be a witness? Imagination accustomed to fill in, fashion symmetry, find the right word. But the right word conveys truth —the wind *seeps* through the leaves, yes, but what does that add to human knowledge other than a tool of communication? What use is it?

Think how your words walk across a vaguely imagined room, a kind of place with no walls to speak of, little or no furniture and what there is only ill-defined, in a mist, perhaps a scrap of vague carpet. What is it *for*?

The reason you can't live from your writing is because you're a bad writer, he thinks suddenly, uninvited words marching into his consciousness. No, not bad, worse than that: just not very good. In truth, more than a tad boring, certainly less than exciting. You have your few moments of glitter but...

So why not die then? Why not die here? Right here. Sit down there on that frozen sofa on that deserted-looking porch over there. Dilapidated grey clapboard house. Sit down there. Huddle in the cold and go the way Ms Dickinson described it, not trying to build a fire, but letting the cold in, first the chill, then the stupor, then the letting go. They say that was the source of the title for Philip Roth's novel. He recites rapidly through freezing lips, *This is the hour of lead/Remembered if outlived/As freezing persons recollect the snow/First the chill, then the stupor...*

*Recollect the snow*, he thinks, and suddenly realizes he is standing still on the sidewalk, gazing across a frozen lawn at the porch of an abandoned house, dilapidated, at a frozen half sunken sofa there. Both his feet are numb and his nose and cheeks and fingers, too. You *could* kill yourself here this way. Take a seat, pal. Take a load off. Recollect the snow. He glances down the long steep hill to the now dim glitz of the avenue. Turns to look up to a lighted building of the campus, perhaps three hundred yards above him. He realizes that he is staring at Noble Hall, the side of the building, the four side windows of the lounge, and vaguely beyond the whisper of the snowy air, he hears music. There is a party in progress there.

Abruptly, he leans into the snow again and begins walking on his numb feet, banging them to make the blood move, past the second graffitied mailbox—*You know what you've done*, thinks of his wife, his sons, you have no right to die, no right.

His eyes burn in the cold and with the bite of snow at his face. His brain is heavy. You *could* have slept there. If you'd sat down you could have slept, you could have died. The thought is exhilarating even in his drowsy state, and part of his mind is forking up lines for a lecture he has been preparing over the past few weeks.

*You want to capture life in words and hope that in so doing you will make it possible to discern reality — truth, perhaps, not to posit too grandiose notions of our functions. Perhaps to erase the line between fic-*

*tion and reality…Trapped in language you seek a door that is not there… seek a door that is not there…*

He is walking along the path to the Noble Hall entryway as he thinks these words, and the music from within grows louder. He hears the words of a song by Counting Crows: *Every time she sneezes I believe it's love and O lord I'm just not ready for this sort of thing…*

Beneath the high ceiling the windows are tall and the air hot. Twomey stands inside the second set of double doors, shivering as the room's heat overpowers the cold of his body. He feels foolish, desperately wishing to ask for help. *Am I frostbit?*

Off to the end of the room, the folding chairs have been taken away, and people dance to some kind of aerobics-sounding music, voices chanting very quickly *Let it all go let it all go*, bodies hiphopping faster than Twomey can follow with his eyes. Against the opposite wall is a snack table. A man Twomey recognizes stands there holding aloft a gallon jug of red wine and declaiming, "Ah the seadark wine!" He fits his nose into the bottleneck, "Vintage cat piss," fills a white plastic cup, inhales, "Not much nose," tastes, grimaces, "Earthy. Death on the middle palate."

The moment of panic passes. Twomey slides off his glasses, studies his flexing fingers. With the skin of his palm, he feels his face, feels the prickling return of warmth and sensation.

He is hungry.

Stuffing his knit cap and gloves into the pockets of his field jacket he goes for the snack table. There is a huge brick of cheddar cheese, ritz crackers, plastic knives, carrots and cucumbers and white dip and a big plastic squeeze bottle of yellow mustard. He is famished, remembers then that he and Burns had eaten nothing beyond the olives in their martinis.

In this state, the cheese is excellent, as is the wine. He stands there munching happily, drinking, his back to the party, windows bumping and rattling in the storm.

He refills his wine cup, doffs his jacket, finds an armchair in the corner. The party is spread across a narrow connecting hallway into the snack bar and rooms beyond—the library and lounge.

Twomey begins to feel conspicuous. His eyes pick through the crowd for familiar faces, see Strayer, the poet director of a program in Ohio. Chinless face in a frizzle of black beard. Strayer was known for having taken up with one of his students, twenty years younger than he. He left his wife and children to take her from her husband, married her, created a teaching slot for her, then instituted a rule in the program whereby faculty-student affairs were cause for firing/expulsion.

At the moment, the gossip went, the second Mrs. Strayer was getting it on with one of *her* students, a young Asian poet from out west.

All that sex, Twomey thinks, and almost immediately his eyes pick out a man and woman standing in a niche beside the double doors that lead to the hall. She is caressing the man's face. Are they lovers? No doubt. Obviously. And both married probably, or at least one of them. The man probably. Yet it seems a vital scene, a scene of life, their silent eyes embracing, her palm on his cheek, and Twomey wonders again why he is so full of shame for that one digression. The other thing was long in the past, before Jenny. He is happy at home. He and Jenny are too good together to risk some meaningless flutter of desire. Hasn't always been that way. Bad times, too. But in the past. He touches the gold band on his finger.

The couple by the door is in shadow. Their faces are indistinct, but he can see they are attractive, well-dressed. The scene seems almost out of a black and white movie. Real life, he thinks, is like something that happens in a black and white film on a big screen between well-dressed men and women in cocktail lounges prior to 1960.

He glances at his watch. Past eleven. The pace of the party has grown serious. Those with intentions are now either focused in or growing desperate. So many divorced couples here looking for new ways to fail. Who are you to judge? Robert Farleigh is now with Evelyn Flynn. Michael Flynn is now with William Happel. Cora Farleigh is now with...

He rises, moves past the silent, grinding embrace at the door into the corridor. In the alcove by the phone booth, a young woman strums a guitar to an audience of three, two men and another young woman, curled up on a two-man sofa. Twomey recognizes her, a very tall very slender blond from California who works as a copy editor at *Vogue*. Her eyes are large and blue and her limbs folded together on the short sofa give her a foetal look, some sort of moonchild foetus, extreme delicacy. The other woman sings an intricate text Twomey is not familiar with. The men watch her attentively, looking useful, fatuous. He glances once again at the tall California girl curled up on the little sofa, remembers her name is Stella. Her skin is so pale, luminous, he can imagine her body glowing naked in the dark, finds himself in a fantasy of kissing her face, becomes aware of himself, steps out of it.

He crosses the snack bar to the library door, on which is hung a sprig of holly sprayed with silver snow and adorned with a gold bow and silver and blue balls. Blue balls, he thinks. In the library is more dancing. The music now is Led Zeppelin. *Hey hey when you walk that way/Watch honey drip/Can't keep away...*

More memories of the sixties. He passes an armchair on which a middle-aged woman sits; a man kneeling before her speaks thickly, "What if I were to fling myself at your feet?"

Twomey turns back. Sees his beachboy student, Serafino, smiles, near desperate for someone to talk to, but the boy disappears. Go to bed, he thinks. But to do so now seems such patent retreat. He turns in a circle watching the talking animals dance, touch, kiss. He drains his glass, heads for the wine jug, notes that the cheese block is smaller now by half—time measured by cheese—and just as he cuts a wedge from it, someone beside him says, "Hi, Frederick Twomey!"

The woman from Julio's, Janet Fallow, and Twomey experiences inordinate joy at seeing her here, greeting him.

"We never actually met," she says. He takes the warm hand she offers. "No," he says. "Hi, good to meet you finally." She reaches into her blouse to adjust her bra strap with a shrug of her shoulder and what could be more alluring than that? Twomey thinks as he offers to pour for her, and she holds out her glass in both hands, saying, "Please, sir," in a way that triggers his blood. His glass is already empty. He refills it, wondering where Burns is. "Geoff get back all right?" he asks, knowing he is asking for it and seeing in her glance he's going to get it.

"We shared a cab up the hill. He was sleepy." Her smile is eloquent, explaining that Geoff was on the silly side but okay. "Loved your reading," she says.

"Thanks. Thanks a lot."

She shakes her head. "That ending. I was just…" She breathes in sharply and touches her chest.

She is so pretty, her mouth, he can't take his eyes from her face, and it embarrasses him, but then he thinks she doesn't seem to mind. Perhaps she is fond of being so pretty. Then he begins to think perhaps she is fond of him, fancies him, and his breath steepens.

"Why is it," he asks, realizing with the question how tight he is even if his voice sounds under control, but deciding to let himself go, "that a man wants a woman with a smile like yours to smile only for him?"

"Because maybe a woman like me likes that," she says.

He kisses her lips and she moves closer, her body light, she offers her tongue. He puts down his wine glass, folds his arms around her, feels her thigh slip between his, and her whisper, "Let's go to my room."

# Chapter Three

The winter light is sharp across the snowy track yard, and Twomey notes his head is not as poisoned as it might have been. The train rolls south out of Montpelier station, carrying him away in his field jacket with a yellow stripe down the back that he could not quite wash off.

His mood is a cocktail of pleasure and self-hatred, his brain buzzes with scraps of music, song couplets, images faceted as cut glass. He is not certain why he hates himself, why he is pleased —rather, he does know; he both hates himself and is pleased in two conflicting directions: because she wanted him, he could have done it, and because in the end, he didn't, because he kissed the side of her throat and whispering an apology stole away from her bed with his pants still buckled.

Half-hearted sinner. If you must sin, sin boldly. Cold feet. Feet it was. His desire freed him of care as he undressed her in her barracks room, within the yellow painted cinderblock walls, but her feet brought him back. The slender firmness of her body dazzled his palms as they slid down her flanks, her legs, to the bottoms of her feet. He was about to go down, final abandon, hovering like a bee mouth above her yellow bloom as the palms of his hands caressed the bottoms of her feet and felt there a thick hard sheet of callous, sharkskin.

She jogs, he thought. Runs to keep trim. An image of her running along a sidewalk to burn away the fat of oral pleasure stopped him. Unmarried, or divorced, preened for solitary pleasure, moving through the garden on hard feet. It made no sense but it woke him from abandon, before the beemouth sipped, with a question: *Can you get AIDS from this?* And with the question the thought of Jenny. He was already, he knew, guilty by Christ's definition, in his heart, but he still had his pants on, he could still pull back, get away undipped, faithful to the letter if not the spirit of his vow. Leaning on his palms above her in the dark he saw the glint of gold on his left hand.

Then his lips were at her ear. "I'm sorry," he whispered. "I can't do this."

Her incredulous mirthless smile. "You're leaving?"

Then, as now, a second voice cursing him for turning away from perhaps the last time in his life such a pretty young woman would just like that want him, while the first voice urged, *Go, don't look back, cut your losses, burn this bridge now while you still have enough left to look Jenny in the eye knowing you almost fell, stumbled, but regained your balance.*

In the hall, in his sock feet, shirt unbuttoned, tails flapping, shoes in his hand and field jacket god knew where, as could only have been ordained, he met his cherub-faced beachboy student, Serafino. They paused, startled, facing one another. *What now? Play the role? Wink? Wince?* But the boy's eyes slid coldly away from him, a judgement he felt he deserved as he padded down the hall to his own room. The unlocked door reminded him they had stopped here on the way to her room to get his bottle of Hennessey which he had neglected to bring with him when he retreated from her. Denied even the solace of brandy. He considered returning for it—*Scuse me, forgot m'booze*—but could not tolerate being *that* much of an asshole on top of it all. So he entered the room and without even switching on the light crawled into bed and fell asleep married to his hand.

In the morning, amidst the post-festum mess in Nobel Lounge he found his field jacket and gloves where he had left them, though someone had painted a thick stripe of dried Gulden's yellow mustard down the back. Janet? Hard to believe, but who else? And if her, thank god he did retreat. But it was hard to believe. Who else then? Burns? Nah. Serafino, the beach boy student? Why? And how would he know it was Twomey's jacket? And how would he know Twomey had not gone through with it anyway? And why should he care either way? No. But what then? Just some coincidence. Prompted by the gods. Perhaps they had meant him to do it the whole way. Sin. Sin boldly. The sinner's prayers are answered first. The just are tried. *Just?* Her mirthless smile. *You're leaving?* You, sir, are an asshole.

The train stops at White Gulch and a few passengers board. A woman carrying a canvas baby crib takes the seat across from Twomey. She removes her red-quilted coat and stuffs it in the overhead rack, then with deft grace lifts the baby from its bag. A girl it looks like, perhaps six months, and the woman discreetly lifts her sweater and brings the baby's face to her breast. Twomey turns away. The sound of the baby's sucking makes him want to look so he closes his eyes. Still a bit dizzy from yesterday's excess, he opens his eyes again and sees the little bald head, mouth pressed against the soft, white, spread-flat globe. The woman's mouth is soft and content, hands touching the child in a way no man can ever touch anything. The baby's hand too curls against her neck and Twomey thinks he can smell the aroma of milk on her breast and feels desire to touch his lips against the curve of her neck. Why? he wonders. To acknowledge her power. She bore that child, feeds it with her body and sits there in a short skirt, thighs in black stockings, how they adorn themselves, her hair in honey braids so fine and shining at the nape, red on her lips, color on the eyelids that all says *Long for me*, and I do, I'll do as you please, a lie, a role, we all lie, as words lie, cutting slices of truth into functioning realities, seduction, charm, invitation, what does any of this mean? What did it mean that Janet Fallow for whatever reason wanted me in her bed, that a conference full of writers filtered down to a party where people gathered for the touch of one another while the sound system spewed out spiritual pollution and that one song *I want to fuck you/I want to fuck you hard/to drive you crazy*, that's what they sing now as he and Janet Fallow made their way up the stairs to her room, his heart giddy with the pleasure of complicity.

Now he sits back against the seat, eyes closed and he rocks with the movement of the train as his mind moves back in the shadow of drink-blurred memory, reconstructing those moments to examine them, constructing images of Janet's body in words —the sweeping line of neck and shoulder, maroon nipples, lean muscle of her belly and the yellow hair where his mouth hovered, tangy aroma...

On the other side of his eyelids he senses the baby growing restive. The gurgling becomes an impatient chatter, a shriek. Twomey's eyes open to see the infant kicking, flailing its chubby arms, and the mother, heavy-eyed, whispers, "*Sh! Sh!*" The baby pauses for an instant, then spits up yellow barf on her cornblue sweater. She reaches for a diaper, wipes herself, places it over the baby's face as if to smother, but only wipes the mouth and chin.

Her eyes are wide, her mouth small. He watches her sidewise. Objectively she is far from beautiful yet there is a beauty in her face, in its tiredness, its triumph over the moment, over herself. The baby is still now, staring into her face. Then its mouth opens, and it spits up again.

"Must be the movement of the train," he says by way of comfort and reassurance.

The young mother nods, firming her lower lip as the baby barfs again, and Twomey's eyes go for the window and the word barfogenic pops into his mind. A barfogenic scene. Barfogenesis. I shall not barf, he chants in his mind to the rhythm of the train slide-bumping across the white landscape, past an old boarded up building. House of gone time. The past. Behind this train somewhere. Land of dreams. Remember she said, "It's not sex I'm after. I can give myself an orgasm any day of the week."

Time measured by cheese. Slowly dwindling, slice upon slice, cut away unto infinity, till nothing remains but...

"You can?" See her doing the Madonna on some bed. Wanna watch me? You bet. "Sure," she says. Her sultry gaze. "A good one." Time measured by orgasms lost, spent. Who was it said you only get so many in a lifetime, the limited number of orgasms theory, thought it was a joke, might be true. Or, *Use it or lose it, Twom*, said Burns in the bar. Use time or lose it. Partake of the great clock of cheese.

At the cheese block he remembers now, as he reached to cut a wedge, one leg suddenly didn't want to do what he directed it to. He dipped, swivelled sharply, looked around to see if anyone had noticed, but the room was filled with drunken people, dancers. He had not yet bumped into her. I didn't do anything. Not really. Her standing there, lithe and slender, as we spoke, standing close to me, and I wondered at some point whether it was a conscious exercise of power, her reeling me in to her. She was like a sea plant and I was underwater in low gravity drifting in to her. Oh, yes, and then it was that Burns appeared again for a blurred instant, smile tainted, or was that a dream fragment? No? Yes? This morning on the chow line in the ugly cinder block canteen his bloated face as you shovelled scrambled eggs onto your plate, and "Well well," says Burns, "if it isn't holier than thou with egg on his plate." Beside him is Ed McPeak whom Twomey knew to be a practising Catholic and whose wife blushed deeply at a faculty party once when Twomey showed up in a tee shirt emblazoned with the words *SAME SHIT DIFFERENT DAY*.

"Should have heard this guy last night preaching about the requisites of fidelity," Burns says over his shoulder to the Catholic McPeak. "I et it raw until I caught his act in the Noble Lounge not two hours later. Way to go, Twom."

Twomey, off balance, murmured, "Ey, Burns, what...?" Burns's smile is furious and McPeak asks, "What was that?"

"In hot embrace. Flagrento delecto, Ed. With a junior female colleague of ours who will here remain nameless."

McPeak's startled face was full of judgement and Twomey too surprised by Burns' fury, laughed it off, hating himself for passivity, putting it out of mind, denying that it bothered him, but feeling now cheated by his friend (ex-friend?) delivering him to McPeak, no doubt a righteous gossip spreading it to how many people now who will have ammunition against Twomey whenever any committee is to decide anything concerning his fate, short or long term. *Professor Twomey is a bit of a rake, is he not? Philanderer. Drinks, too, I've heard. Should have seen him at the NWP. Is that the sort of image we want to promote for the department?*

You bastards. Look into your own hearts! Everyone always checking on what everyone else is doing.

*Got my eye on you, Twomey. Some night last night, ey? Really knocking them down. Two fisted. Got yourself a cozy time with old Janet there, ey boy?*

Hey, *nothing* happened.

*Ha ha.*

Tally it all up. Hold information as a weapon against each other and let you know they know. Hide behind the offense. *I'm safe. I got something on you.* I do not want to live like this. Who was it said, To be a gossip shows an intense interest in gaining knowledge of the world around you and an equally intense disinterest in gaining a knowledge of yourself. Spring that on them next time, save it in your pocket to lash back with.

And that was that NWP Convention. What did you accomplish? Made a few contacts. Picked up a few new titles to read. Gave a public reading of one of your new stories. Delivered your paper on the creation of reality by language and angle, the ego as lens, filter, the imperfect eyes, tempered by Einstein's statement that the idea of fragmentation presumes a wholeness from which it is perceived.

And time can be measured by cheese. The recollection of cheese past.

It is pleasant to sit on this train flying across the snowscape, warm in here and the blueing day outside dying in the distance. I did nothing almost. I was desired by an attractive woman much younger than myself. Tell Jenny. Never. Nothing happened and it's over. Contradiction there. He considers it. *Nothing happened and it's over.* Spine-sprung sentence. Routinely he reaches into the bag at his feet for his notebook, to jot it down and becomes aware of himself, his thoughts, the journey, this moment, the mother across from him, his thoughts of the night before, pleasure of the Janet interlude complicated by guilt toward Jenny and fear toward Burns and McPeak. Has he lost Burns's friendship over this? Or was he ever really a friend? Twomey recalls an incident three-four years ago when he entered a novella contest. The person responsible for the first screening sent him a letter in which she said, *Despite your entry's very considerable literary merits the screening panel has not selected it as a finalist although we would like you to know it came very close.* An unusual letter. Then he learned that Burns was the final judge, and it became clear to him that Burns had asked her to write that letter, that the novella very likely *was* amongst the ten finalists and that Burns, rather than have to be seen *not* to select Twomey's novella, or to avoid having to declare himself unable to judge because he knew Twomey, or even out of an unwillingness to let Twomey win, contrived to get out of it like that. Or on the other hand, it could also have been that Burns thought his entry shit, but wanted to throw him a bone of special attention. Could've been that, too. Twomey put it out of mind, considered it a clumsy attempt by Burns to be discreet. But wished the man might have given him the respect of being direct, tell him to his face, *Fred, I'm sorry but out of the ten I just didn't feel I could pick yours. There were others which to my taste were better.* How would I have reacted? Fairly? Or with bitterness? Is this as far as friendship goes? No further? Or is it even friendship? And what *is* friendship? Do you know? Have you ever?

For a moment he puzzles over an observation espied in the situation. The abuse of language. Guile and cunning. Flattery—one of Dante's circles of hell—which? Enslavement to words. Use them to create a definition of reality to escape: *You* say *this* to him and then *I* won't have to say *that* to him with the result that I don't have to risk being hurt by being honest, he is none the wiser, and you can sit back and know this in your private heart, smiling secretly if it suits you. Twomey thinks of Byron: *You have the letters Cadmus gave/Think you he meant them for a slave?* Slave of your own deceit. Write about it. Put your pen to the page and see what it tells you about all this.

He opens the spiral pad and thumbs forward toward a blank page, scanning his mind for where to begin to record, perhaps *time measured by cheese, slicing upon slicing unto infinity til nothing remains save cheddar crumbs.* Picture Janet Fallow in her solitary sack, fingers on the button, practising the one-handed cut. The thought fires him so for an instant he wonders if he will have to use the water closet to be free of it, but it flares past. Outside the train, an empty brick station flies by, a cozy white church, plasticville style. He remembers a dream in which a boy jumps off a wharf onto him where he dogpaddles, treading, in dark water. They sink together, he fears drowning, wakes.

His fingers come to the blank pages in his spiral pad. He jots in the date. Then his eyes catch on the final words of the preceding day's entry. Printed in green block letters:

*YOU KNOW WHAT YOU ARE AND YOU KNOW WHAT YOU'VE DONE*

*THE FUTURE DOESN'T DESERVE YOU. AND YOU DON'T DESERVE A    FUTURE*

Words he did not put there. For he made no entry yesterday. And he does not own a pen with green ink.

Out the window, the white fields stretch as far as he can see, blending into the white horizon.

## Shadow King

The song on the car radio transforms the winter landscape. Clang of guitars overpowering the leaden sky. Their rhythm drives into your blood as you sit behind the wheel of the old Impala waiting for the light to change on Sunrise Highway, and everything is good again. With elation, you remember your dream, your plan. The long time of empty darkness is behind you. Now the True Will shows itself.

It is hard to believe sometimes, but if you truly consider it, how can you deny? A wave of evil has been sent against you. Before you ever saw the light of being in the world, a hand wished to destroy you. The only defense is to reverse the wave, now, all these years later, and leave the time of empty darkness behind.

The thin sole of your shoe teases the accelerator, beating time, and you glance at the woman in the car beside you, a dark-haired, full-lipped woman in middle age, at the wheel of a BMW.

You sing softly to her, accompanying the radio, through the side window:

> *All your life*
> *Is just a shame shame shame*
> *All your love*
> *Is just a dream dream dream...*

She glances at you, looks quickly away again, but not before you note those dark curls framing her face. You know what they are for. You smile, feel power in your thigh, your eyes, as the amber light flashes, and you gun the motor, considering. If she looks again. You watch from the edge of your vision. Decide your fate, lady. The light is green. Her Beamer rolls out, carries her head of black curls and plump face off to some other destiny.

Okay. That's cool.

You slide the Chevy into first, go left at the next corner, thinking of something to write in your journal. Write, Call me X. No, write: Call me Xmial. Being a man of letters now. *Je m'appele X.*

The name on the car registration is Alan Angel, not his own either, but that hardly matters. Names are cheap. You can have all the names you need, a man of many names and many parts, but these days it is amusing, in private, in the intimacy of thought, to call yourself X. Both like a slave whose ancestry was lost in the past, a white X, white nigger, but also for another, more private reason that might be told, if and when the time comes, for ironic effect. You never gave me your name, daddy.

Turns of fate. Yes. Existence as we know it is full of sorrow. Every man is a condemned criminal only he does not know the hour of his execution. Words of the true master, the Great Beast, the true Shadow King. Yet the wheels grind with purpose. Every gesture, every movement sets the scene, decides the course, achieves the unknown schedule. The long process of evolution moves on to its unknown conclusion in this darkness, and each man plays his role. Nothing is coincidence, not when you have found your True Will and the Nuctemeron: Light issuing from the darkness. There is only synchronicity.

For example: You enter a doorway to get out of the rain. Find it's a library. You check out the computer to pass time. Key in the name you know like poison from the baby blue letter she left you, red ink on flimsy baby blue paper in a baby blue envelope with a scalloped flap, sealed on the spit from her very mouth. *Ipsissimus. To My Son,* in flowing letters on the front, as if anyone could know what the fuck that meant, who the fuck her son was, what the fuck her name was when she was too stupid to write it on the envelope before she ate the dark.

But fate do make its turns. The baby blue letter was sent on by someone who worked it out, found its way into his palm. His thumb slit the spit-sealed flap, and there amidst all the red curling words on the four flimsy blue pages was The Name. Name of the fucking father. And of the son. Same name as there in the library on a rainy Des Moines Street one chilly wet April day, the name keyed into the computer for the hell of it, you thought, to pass time, then your thumb, same thumb as slit the flap on the envelope, that thumb *knew* something, thumb that was a claw eons ago, when we crawled on bellies and four feet, thumb hit enter and

*blip*

*blip*

*blip*

*blip*

suddenly you got information you never had before, suddenly you see it all there, access to the past, in great detail. Followed by: a plan. Action. Redress. Right the balance. Reverse the wave of evil. The angel with the sword points the way: East.

Double-em: all your life is just a dream dream dream.

You cruise slowly down the street of large brick houses, checking them out. One in particular, deep lawn, apple trees, the large front window like a screen, the screen of a coming drama, coming attractions, but grey now as this grey afternoon, and the feeling in your head, behind your face has such a purity to it. Who could argue with that? This is holy. Angel and demon join hands and the fate that was a secret seed, lost among the years, now blooms its dark.

You take the next left, follow for a mile, then left again, down a street of identical three-level three-family houses. You park outside the fifth of them, residence of Alan Angel, aka X, aka Xmail, aka... You find that out when the time is in, Daddy cool. The number on the house is 123. And that's how simple it'll be: 1-2-3. With proper ritual and the help of the masters.

In the trunk are two large brown paper sacks that you lift out and carry to the side door, your entrance, which you open with a key, balancing one bag on your hip. Up the stairs to your lousy two rooms. Check the threads you plastered across the door. Intact. Unlock it and check the five scraps of paper on the floor arranged in an inverted triangle. Just so. Intact.

When you know what you're about you know how to go about it. Write that down among the meditations, the record you keep of this, the journal. But real cautious like. Code. Only you have the key. The flowers were lovely today means you know what, and Double-em is you know who. Concentrate. Remember. We have the history of a potentially important event here. Reversal of the tides of malevolence initiated against an innocent who shall now shift it back to the crooked one who goes among the righteous.

Set the paper bags on the spattered formica table in the kitchen area, lift out a quart bottle of chocolate milk, a package of frankfurters, a loaf of white bread, a copy of The National Enquirer. Check out the headline: Suburban Witch Coven: Blood Sacrifice. Your eye rests there as your mind listens to the thoughts offered from the Angel. Meditation: *The best blood is of the moon, monthly. Then the fresh blood of a child, then of enemies. Then of the priest or of the worshippers, last of some beast.* Your eye holds in the black letters on white, mass of dots, in the depth of timelessness. You know this place, have trained yourself to accept its appearance, receive its trance when offered, when consciousness lifts away to open the gates of the world behind the veil of matter. Now you don't need to think; thought thinks you, informs you that your soul wandering in the darkness soon will find the limitless light once the hostile current against you has been reversed upon its author.

It is a task set for you by your sacred Angel.

*What must I do?*

You will know.

The black letters before your eyes become words again, the objects on the kitchen board enter your vision and you are your consciousness once again. You breathe once, deeply, and are calm. Slowly, calmly, you scan the room, drawings and masks on the walls, the pine shelves, the sleek spines of your books—*BOOK FOUR, KING OF THE SHADOW REALM*, fable, myth, poetry, *AN AMERICAN PRAYER*... A crack in the wall plaster beside the closet door draws your gaze. The crack runs like a thread from a bashed-in hole the size of a silver dollar. Lift the marker from your shirt pocket, print meticulously in iodine red around the hole and along the crack, above and below, Dancing dancing on the edge of this dancing dancing on the edge of this dancing... It fits exactly six times and ends in perfect symmetry, completion. You stare at the words for several moments, smiling, before you turn away again, satisfied.

From the other bag, you remove a copy book with a marbleized cover, a manila envelope, a box of neatly sharpened Number 3 Ticonderoga pencils, a pack of looseleaf paper. Something in your mind. Music. Violins. You go to the tape player, find Sacre du Printemps, music of that time you thought so old now truly modern, days when the Great Beast walked the earth, recording his system. Pack the books and supplies into the beat-up attaché case you lifted from beneath the counter of the coffee shop (nothing worth nothing in it, but the case was nice, looked sincere). Check your watch. Too early. Too light still.

Sit in the lumpy armchair by the window, staring out over the sloping backyards, yellow winter grass in square segments of chain-link fence, angling down over a littered field to the highway. Waiting is a dangerous time, a test of faith, a time when chaos might shed the order you have placed upon it and become mere chaos again. The wildness is filled with demons who would trick you, blind you, block you from knowing. God himself, the greatest of all demons, seeks to trick the threatening mind of the magician with True Will.

As an exercise, require yourself to sit straight in your chair, lift your feet from the ground. Practice mastery. Doubt is fat, slack. You are the master.

Slowly lower your feet to the floor again. From beneath the chair, remove the little carton in which four slim notebooks are stored, three marbleized copy books and one spiral bound with a brown cover. It bothers you slightly that they are not uniform. Not thinking clearly when you started. Maybe take the time to copy out the meditations in the spiral book to one that matches the others. Is that irrelevant? Hold the books on your lap in a neat stack, run your fingers over the covers, along the edges. You do not have to open them. You know what is written on the pages, know what all the words mean. No one else would understand certain things there, written backwards, in stagger code, with other secret encryptions.

Anyone wishing to learn your secrets would have to employ a cryptographer. If it ever comes to that. You will be gone before they have time to respond. On to other adventures. Leaving behind only your signature, irrefutable but uninterpretable. It will appear again, staggered about the country. Will be known and feared.

See the ghost of your own face reflected in the window, suspended over the yellow segmented yards sloping down toward the highway. Your face like a disembodied wafer of yellowish grey. Smiling.

Lift your feet again, sit that way until it hurts, and keep on longer, suspended, as the grey afternoon air darkens. Check the watch again. Carefully lower your feet, return the books to their carton, the carton back beneath the chair. From the closet in the hall, take the long black nylon satchel, loop the strap over your shoulder. Now rearrange the paper triangle, reversed this time, and with spit from your mouth paste threads across door and jamb before locking it. With your fist trace a sacred x in the air across the door, blowing into each of its invisible angles.

And now the time is right for the next gambit, your legs strong jogging down the stairs to your Chevy.

# Chapter Four

Twomey bikes through the long shadows of late winter afternoon, his ancient Raleigh rattling over clumpy snow. First day of the final segment of the semester, and he surprised himself with an impulse. Ten minutes into his last, double session, after explaining the texts and requirements, he said, "One more thing I will require this term: that you write. Now get out of here. Go home and do it. Or to whatever your favorite, most fecund place for doing that may be and do it. Go and write and bring back what you've written with you next time. You will be required to read it out. See ya!"

And he was out of there, locked his office, grabbed his bike, thinking of the fact that Larry and Jimbo were away in Washington on a class trip, that Jenny Jenny Jenny was home alone, that she might just be in the mood to give him a little, that even if she wasn't, he might be able to ply her with liquor.

And there is no law against him thinking a little bit about Janet Fallow's spicy bush while he is at it.

He arcs the bike around a snow heap and into the driveway, glances at his next door neighbor's shiny new T-bird. Red. Thinks, It is not possible for an American male who does not own a shiny new red T-bird not to be envious of one who does. Leo Zilka steps out of the car, a broad-shouldered man with a big nose and high cheekbones, constant five o'clock shadow. He waves to Twomey, who lifts a hand from his handlebars to wave back and swings his leg down from the bike. He and Jenny and Zilka and his wife used to dine together every couple of months; then Zilka and Pauline got divorced. Now Leo only comes over in the afternoon to pour out his sorrow to Jenny over endless cups of tea.

*You're too kind, Jenny. Don't let him use your time like that.*
*What are neighbors for, Fred?*

Twomey lifts the garage door, locks his bike. In the house, he can hear the upstairs shower, contemplates shucking his duds, creeping in with her. Bad idea. Jenny doesn't like surprises. Instead he goes to the booze cart, shakes a martini, kicks off his shoes to sit, feet up, on the red sofa and waits. At the edge of the room is her studio annex, where she does the light work, the finishing touches. A sheet covers her latest creation, which he has yet to see, a mysteriously clunky, floor-lamp-looking shape under a shroud. Upstairs the shower has stopped. Let her come down naked, please. Just in underpants. Or a robe that can be easily removed. Let her be horny as me. As I.

He hears her light step jogging down the stairs, along the hall, and she appears, alas, fully dressed, in a white smock over striped tights. He watches for a moment, realizes she hasn't seen him yet. She stares out the window, funny smile on her mouth, light in her eyes.

He says, "What does that smile mean?" and she gasps, hand flying to her breast. She freezes, then melts in fury: "You scared the *shit* out of me, you idiot!" Her fury makes him jump so he spills his martini in his crotch, sets down his glass, moving toward her, laughing, apologizing, but she can see right through the maneuver and stiff arms him away as he gets closer.

"No way," she says. "I've been waiting all day to get some studio time in."

"You take a shower before you paint?"

"Has it taken all these years for you to notice?"

He shrugs. "Well, Neruda always washed his hands before writing." He's at the liquor cart. "Want one?"

"Not yet," she says. "You're *early.*"

"Well, excuse me, do I have to apply to come home early? I decided to set them free two hours early so I could come home and seduce you."

"Not a chance, buddy."

She's at her shrouded clunky floor lamp thing now, but glances back, funny look in her eye. "Oh, did you see Geoff Burns?"

"Yeah, in school, a few hours ago."

"No, here, he just left. You must've just missed him."

"What'd he want?"

"You. Said he wanted to ask you something."

Twomey's mind is working: To ask me what? Could've asked at school. He glances sidewise at Jenny. To tell her something maybe. About what happened (didn't happen) in Vermont? No. If he'd done that Jenny would've confronted me already. Frontal attack. What then? Cryptic insinuations? Why? Why the fuck would he do that? Get this out of your mind. You're just a slithering bucket of guilt. Catholic heritage. Nothing happened in Vermont. At the end of the day, nothing happened. Get that straight in your Catholic apostate head.

Fresh drink in hand, the spilt booze drying in his crotch, he asks, "Mind if I watch you work?"

"Sure."

"Sure you mind? Or sure it's okay?"

"The latter."

Twomey works a little, too. Lifts out of himself, standing by the window, imagining.

Above and behind the house, the sky is the blank white of an empty movie screen. Winter darkness gathers along the street, across the lawn, at the walls and windows. Mother night wraps softly about like a hand of mist.

Someone standing beneath the crooked bare limbs of the apple trees at the edge of the property or the magnolia in the center could watch the house unseen now, observe the long rectangle of yellow light at the picture window, a shadow moving behind it, a woman, Jenny.

Lithe and graceful, she removes a sheet from an object in the middle of the room and stands contemplating it: A cage on the seat of a dilapidated wooden armchair. The bars of the cage are elegant, hand-crafted wood, lacquered silver and gold; within them, seated on a tiny chair resembling the one on which the cage itself sits is a doll, the likeness of a pudgy infant, its posture at once merry and threatening, its eyes red, teeth bared.

She steps around the chair, pauses, head cocked, looks at the

51

sketch pad in her hands, redirects an outline.

"Another in the series of evil baby dolls, ey?" Twomey says.

She makes a noncommittal noise in her throat.

"What's the title?" Twomey asks. He sits now across the room at the corner of the red sofa, stocking feet flat in the elephant-foot print of a large Persian carpet, a textbook on the art of fiction open on the sofa beside him. He holds a cocktail glass by the stem, watching the line of his wife's body as she moves. *Light as a dancer*, he thinks, agreeably high on the first half of his second martini of a late Friday afternoon, the second half of the first now forgotten.

"Baby Doll in Cage with Red Eyes and Teeth," she says without looking at him.

"You can tell it's Mattel: It's swell," he says. "Is it a boy doll or a girl doll?"

"All they gave it in the way of a sex was a smudge."

"Well you're an artist. Create sex for it."

That loose white smock, striped tights, tease his imagination, and he watches her with martini-primed, leisurely desire. Thank god for that class trip. No kids for two days. The quiet ornamentations of Miles Davis and John Coltrane pulsing from the stereo, blowing "So What?" the gin and vermouth seeping brightly into his brain.

It excites him, thinking about what she will do with the figure she is creating. In a while, today, next week, next year, it will appear in some transformed manner as a sculpture or a picture. He ponders how much more methodical she is about her art, worries for a moment whether he is a charlatan, forces the fear away as a threat to his admiration of his wife's talent. With a lazy desire he looks forward to fulfilling later, he watches her move. It is a simple afternoon, he thinks. Simple pleasures. A day to feel love. A harbor in the vast and varied oceans of their eighteen years together.

On the parquet floor before one of the stereo speakers sits their cat, Nicola, black with a white throat and paws, staring curiously into the speaker. She slaps at it with one paw. Twomey contemplates her there, wonders what goes on in the mind, the brain of a cat.

"You think cats think?" he asks.

"I think you think cats think. I think they just are."

52

"Well look at her there. She's actually *contemplating* that speaker. She's trying to figure it out. But when she takes a jump, you know, you see how she measures it, how she takes in all the parameters. She looks like a computer. With those weird eyes. *O such grace is wasted on a cat/If but my soul could walk like that.*"

"Gooey."

Actually he is thinking of his wife, the way *she* moves. He cannot even hear the sound of it she is so light and graceful, the only woman he has ever been able to dance with. She could follow anyone.

"I wish you would come over here so I could get to know you a little bit better," he says; then, glancing at the window, "Hey! It's snowing!" Large flakes fall steadily outside the window. He rises, steps across the parquet floor to look out. A shadow slips from beneath the magnolia to the apple trees, is gone. Or was it there at all? The image is fleet as thought, the thought slips away. He stands there blinking, peering at the deepening darkness beneath the trees, around the houses across the way, his neighbors with their strange secrets and private lives. Me with my secret from Vermont, Janet. Burns with his secret affairs. *Does your wife know, Geoff? In a way, I think she does.* He considers the people who live in the neighboring houses here, behind blind windows, in the shelter of tall dark pines. The quiet drab woman whose father has translated Baudelaire and Cocteau. She was a guest here at dinner one evening and didn't speak all night while her husband, who is an electrical contractor, spoke at great length about world politics; he was incensed about things the US had not done, that we had not continued into Baghdad and taken out Saddam Hussein when we had the chance, that mark his words one day soon we would have to go back and finish the job, that we had not bombed the Serbs, had not taken out their cannon positions over Sarajevo: "It's such precision," he kept saying. "Bing bing bing, they're out of the game, those bastards!" In the squat brick house next to theirs lives the thick-lipped pathologist and his wife with their three overweight children. The pathologist is a merry fellow, always has a joke, a ready smile, always eager to join you for a drink, and he spends his days slicing up corpses. The man from the Egyptian Embassy in the house next to that; he will not allow his daughter to

53

have a bicycle. Twomey gave her one that his youngest boy Larry had outgrown and the father made her return it — maybe because it was a boy's bike? Diplomatic error on Twomey's part there, not to have asked the father first. And two houses down, the bright-eyed old woman you'd think was a classic American grandmother, but who lives alone with her cats and her Christmas tree that she never takes down, sits in a chair with cats in her lap, around her feet, and watches old Christmas films over and over, Wonderful Life, Miracle on 34th Street, The Christmas Carol.

He considers the lives of these people. Civilized people. Middle class. Educated. And how do they live behind their masks and disguises? Twomey heard a story a few weeks before about a professor of history who lives down the street, a professor who taught Twomey at C.C.N.Y. years before and who, Twomey was told, keeps locks on his refrigerator, telephone and television; his wife and children are not permitted access to these appliances when he is not present. And Burns blithely cheats on his wife. And you almost did, too. Confess it? Get it out of the way. Ask her forgiveness. Don't go there. No.

He lifts his eyes to the falling snow which cheers him as it has always done, all his life, since childhood. Please don't let it stop. The flakes fall steadily, pretty as a picture, big white dots against the dark. He glances across at the trees again, blinks, wonders, looks into his half empty cocktail glass: What, pray tell, sir, is the function of the remainder of that glass?

He steps across to the booze cart, tongs ice cubes from chrome bucket to chrome shaker.

"What are you doing?" Jenny asks.

"Getting sodden toward sundown."

"Alone?"

His pulse ticks. Alcohol and sex. I love you, Jen. Today I can love in the simplest way, thank god for it. And he turns up a second cocktail glass. "You want a cocktail?" Pours gin with happy abandon into the ice of the shaker as Miles Davis slides off explaining the hidden complexities of "So What?" to the wail of a Coltrane counterpoint, and from the wall, an ornately-framed nineteenth century lithograph of an idiot head globe stares across at the white-throated black cat on its haunches before the black speaker, two mysteries in confrontation (Title: Cat Meets Music?), in turn watched by the lifeless red eyes of the doll being studied by Jenny who, for her part, is studied with desire by Twomey in the grip of simple lechery.

As he hands her the lovely glass, her fingertips touch the back of his hand in an unmistakable gesture. He catches his breath as their eyes meet, their faces moving closer while Twomey's brain sings, And my heart was beating like mad and I said yes, I said yes yes yes...

The only light in the room is from the snow. They lie in one another's arms on a sheet thrown across the expensive living room carpet. Twomey snores lightly, happily, glazed eyes half open. He wakes. Jenny's cheek rests on his chest, light as snow, as feathers. I'm so lucky, he thinks, runs his palm over the silken skin of her neck. At the center of the room, in the shadows, snowlight glints on the red-eyed baby's teeth. The cat is curled up on the black marble window ledge, staring out into the evening. She turns her head back to look at Twomey, her strange green eyes round and wide. Twomey blinks, and the cat's inscrutable eyes narrow in acknowledgement.

His gaze wanders down toward Jenny, and he flinches to see her eyes wide open, watching him. Smiling, she blinks like a cat. "Got my eye on you," she says, and he feels exposed, feels she can see what he almost did in Vermont, that damned intuition, but moves fast to cover his guilt. "Oh, yeah? And I got my eye on you, baby, and I like what I see." He lays his palm over her breast, feels the response of his blood. "So beautiful," he whispers.

"They're just lumps of fat and tissue," she says.

"But so nicely turned." He dips his mouth to her and her fingers lace into his hair. His palm glides down her spine, the velvet-covered muscle and cartilage and bone. He touches the protruding blade of bone at her hip and involuntarily remembers the callus beneath Janet's feet, thinks of Geoff Burns again. For what purpose was he here? To insinuate? Plant little seeds of doubt in Jenny? Why? Remember his odd behavior on the breakfast line, the things he said to McPeak. Imagine if Burns told Jenny about him and Janet. No doubt without mentioning his own philosophy about cheating—not to cheat yourself of pleasure. Maybe a pre-emptive strike is needed here.

He can feel that Jenny doesn't have appetite for a second bout. Neither does he particularly.

"How was the meeting in Vermont, by the way?" she asks. "You haven't said a word about it."

Twomey's pulse lifts. Did Burns say something? "It was strange," he says.

"What was?"

"Geoff Burns. You think you know someone, then suddenly..."

Jenny is up on her elbow now. She reaches for a plastic bottle of diet Pepsi standing on the floor beside where they lay, unscrews the cap, takes a swig. "What happened with Geoff? What did he do?"

"Well he didn't actually do anything as far as I know. But he told me, well, his philosophy of marriage. And apparently he considers it perfectly okay to take what he can get on the side. At least that's what he professes."

Jenny's eyes are level on him, searching his face. He reaches across for a hit of her Pepsi, puts it back, and she is still watching him. He does not know what he will say if Burns has told her, if she confronts him with it. Her gaze is fixed on his, and he wants to lower his eyes, but instead tilts his head, an unvoiced question.

"Is that how you'd like it to be?" she asks.

"What?"

"To be free? To have others?"

This is easy. The exam question you'd hoped for. "No way. Absolutely not."

She is still watching him. "You're sure?"

*Does she know?* He holds up his ring finger, touches the glinting metal. "That's pure gold, Jen. Like you. You're the only woman for me. You're the only one."

And with a purr of affection, she hides her face against his chest. He whispers, singing in her ear, "*Love me two times, ba-abe...,*" but she slips away, murmurs sounds that say no, which makes him wonder. She hadn't seemed to come. *Is she tired of me? Putting up with me?*

"Be good boy now," she whispers and rests her cheek back on his chest again.

He dozes, wakes again to the same room, same scene, same light, his wife's face light on his chest, her mouth open and wet against him. The sensation is pleasing. He slides his palm down over her bottom, and her thigh nudges between his, and without warning a short story begins to write itself in his mind:

*My name is Daniel Fleet. I'm fifty years old, teach college English, love martinis, can still kip into a handstand on the parallel bars. I lift weights in the basement three times a week to keep my wife interested. I've been lucky. She's a dish. She's five years my junior and smarter and more talented than me, but I'm cagier and I have words on my side—she's an artist, all she has is color and form—so that evens us up some. She can be a pain in the butt, but who can't? and maybe once a month I'm ready to walk on her, but you get to recognize the rhythms of your own erratic heart, you get to know that every seventh wave is slightly bigger than the ones that came before, you know that if you don't stand fast somewhere, sometime, you will never be...*

The voice falters to a stop. He cannot tell whether the story is going to be any good or even whether it is anything more than a scrap of voice, but the voice feels convincing, and he knows that feel, knows he might be cheating himself of a good piece of work if he doesn't get up now and write it down.

Jenny's thigh moves, which stirs him, but he can tell she is not quite awake.

"Be right with you," he whispers and slips from her embrace, rises, pictures himself stepping naked along the runner in the hall, how he might look to an observer, flesh of belly and butt assaulted by gravity, his penis bobbing upward (*penis or dick?* he wonders. *A prick by any other name is a cock, schlong, hammer, slammer, wailer...still the same old meat, let's call a spade a shovel*)—his prick bobbing upward.

He gives the image a title, Fifty-year-old Man with Hard-on and Gravity and Head Full of Words.

In his little back office, he rummages in the junk on his desk for a pad and pen, scribbles down the paragraph he has memorized, waits for a moment to see if the voice will bring him more, writes:

*Actually my life is not unlike my father's, despite my early rebellion. Even the surface differences begin now to take on a resemblance to the details of his life. he was an insurance executive who wrote poetry married to a high school art teacher. I teach English and write the occasional story and am married to an artist. Like his, my marriage has lasted. He had two sons, I have two sons. We both started our families later in life, although my youth was more confused than his and I narrowly escaped a disastrous early union. Both of us registered Democratic, although it always has puzzled and troubled me that he once told me supported Joe McCarthy and voted for Richard M. Nixon in 1960...*

The voice falters again. Too much information. Fleetingly he thinks of writing about a man who cheats on his wife and has to carry that guilt around with him, but he rejects the thought and wonders whether his own guilty conscience will now grow into a censoring voice and has a flash of insight: censors are guilt-ridden. They censor what they want to hide of themselves. He writes that down, waits for more, but nothing comes.

Naked in his swivel chair, he stares at his bulletin board, a messy collage of snapshots, clippings, quotes. His eye falls on one, something his oldest son, Jimbo, said many years before when he was perhaps nine or ten and Twomey read him Robinson's "The House on the Hill": *They have all gone away/The house is closed and still/There is ruin and decay/In the house on the hill/There is nothing left to say..."*

"Well what do you think of that, Jimbo?" Twomey asked, and the boy said, very serious, "I think you could get the house fixed up, Dad."

He looks at those words, remembering the sweet young face of the boy as he spoke them, and his eyes trail across the little display of old photographs in antique frames on the spindle-legged writing desk which is the only piece of furniture salvaged from his childhood home.

He thinks then of his mother, rather evades the thought of her, fifteen miles away, alone in her apartment, her memory and consciousness fading like a faded photograph.

As his mind drifts over these thoughts, Twomey hears, or thinks he hears, the sound of his garage door slamming, followed by footsteps in the alley. Or is it the neighbor? He switches off the lamp and peers out the curtain. It is still snowing, which cheers him, but the snow is not sticking to the alley so no footprints are visible—if there were any. He looks to either side of the window, can see nothing.

He looks at the pad on his desk again. The voice is gone. He frowns. It occurs to him that everything he has written, aside from the name in the first sentence and the regularity of his gym visits, is straight out of his own life.

Sometimes putting simple things into words makes them seem more real to him. Why? he wonders. In a sense, he thinks, stumbling into something he will likely use later on his students, man is *trapped* in language.

He chucks the pad back into the rubble of papers, returns along the hall runner to the living room, whispering, "My life's the poem I would have writ/I could not both live and utter it." Or rather, "My life's the thing I could not live/I was too busy writing."

"Ah, the writing life," he says softly, knowing he is speaking only to himself unless Jenny poses a question about what he's said. She has lit half a dozen candles along the window ledge and she sits on a footstool studying her caged doll in the flickering light. It is not really very long since she has started trying to be an artist, after many years of thinking about it, little forays into works never completed, and Twomey feels certain she will have success at it, far more than the very limited recognition he has for his writing. She is more patient than he, more methodical. He is all instinct. He understands nothing, never has, he knows instinctively that he must not understand, he must merely feel when he writes or it dies on him.

"Did you hear something before?" he asks.

"Like what?"

"I don't know."

At the window, he can see the snow is now sticking to the lawn and the branches of the trees, layering the tops of fences and parked cars.

He stands there, sleepy-eyed, in the flickering candlelight imagining how he would look from the lawn, the street, naked-chested middle-aged man in candlelight.

The headlights of a car sweep past, blink out at the far foot of the lawn. He watches, city-boy alert, sees something, thinks he sees something, the lights again, an image, blinks, nothing.

What he saw, what he thought he saw, for a split second...to become a literalist of the imagination... Ever since he started wearing bifocals every tree stump was a crouched animal. Jenny reads his thoughts—or his posture maybe—squinting geezer.

"You saw something," she says, circling her sculpture once again.

"An imaginary toad in a real garden."

"What?"

"I saw something."

"What?"

"I saw a figure in a red robe carrying a sword and wearing the head of an animal, an antelope I think."

"You saw this?"

"There was a light—like the brights of a car, and then this figure. I blinked and it was gone."

"You *saw* this."

He sips his drink, stares at the empty black lawn, feeling the eyes of his wife, turned from her sculpture, studying him. "No," he says, sips again, already having sorted the image to its only possible sources—bad eyes, facility for producing concrete thought images, hundred-proof blue Cork gin in his martinis.

Then as he looks again, a figure appears on the street, turns toward the house.

"Hey!" he says. "It's Jimbo! What's Jimbo doing home?"

Jenny is already pulling on her tights while Twomey searches for his underwear. The bell rings.

"You dressed?" Jenny asks and clicks on the overhead light, moving toward the door as Twomey zips his black jeans and pulls a black teeshirt over his head. Cold air rushes in as the door opens. "Where's your key, young man?"

"Forgot it," Jimbo says, tall and slouched and big-nosed.

Twomey chuckles. *Thank god for small favors.* "What're you doing home anyway?" he asks. "You're supposed to be in Washington."

"I didn't feel good. Got off the bus."

His mother is all over the boy now, reaching up to feel his brow and cheek, while Twomey notes a twinge of annoyance (jealousy?) inside himself, puzzling over an idea that there's something wrong with the time frame here. *When* did he get off the bus? How exactly did he get back and from where and what's he been doing since? *Drop it, Twomey, give the kid a break.*

"What's wrong, honey?" Jenny asks. "You don't feel warm."

"Bad stomach. I'm okay. Just didn't feel like feeling lousy in a hotel all weekend."

"Did Larry go ahead?"

"Yeah. I'm gonna lay down."

"Don't you want some tea and toast?"

"No, thanks, I'm fine."

Twomey watches the boy, tall and slim, his nose still a little too large for his face which has not grown as quickly as the rest of him, his teeth and jaw large and strong. The boy disappears up the stairway, and involuntarily Twomey thinks of his own older brother, as he does whenever he glimpses, or thinks he glimpses, some weakness in his older son. Jimbo was named for Twomey's older brother, a fact which had grown terrifying for Twomey, for when the boy was five, too old for a name change, his eponymous Uncle James turned a 30/30 against his own forehead and with a plastic Chinese backscratcher molded to look like clenched fingers, pressed the trigger. The wound was star-shaped, and all the music in Jimbo's head went out with his brain, for he had never learned to write down the notes. Twomey's palm lifts to his eyes. We have not lived right, he thinks, wondering what he means, but he wrenches his mind from the image rising to consciousness. He looks out the window, at the white snow, the lightening lawn, looks at his wife, her cute black curls, her lovely grey eyes.

"Well," he says, "so much for the love nest."

She moves close to him and lays a palm on his chest. "We *do* have a bedroom. With a door. That can be shut."

"What if I can't again? You know, men can't just fake it like women can." And he curses himself as her eyes jolt and go cool. "You think I fake it?"

"Jenny, it was a joke."
"Well, it was a stupid joke."

# Chapter Five

In the dream he hears someone in the hall outside his door. He hears the familiar squeak of the doorknob being turned, but the door does not open. He sits up in bed, clicks on the lamp. Nothing. Jenny is not in bed. He is in a single bed in a room from some other time, some other life.

*Who's there?* he calls in a whisper. *Who is it?* Nothing. He gets out of bed. *Who is there?* The knob is turning again. It must be someone in the family he thinks, but why don't they answer. Then he sees the door is open, and standing there is someone he has never seen before. A strange-looking man with a narrow pinched face, wearing camouflage clothes. At first he looks like someone frail and unimpressive, someone he could shove aside with one arm. He feels rage build in him at this intrusion, that a complete stranger should take the liberty of entering his life in this way, his house, his bedroom.

"Who the *fuck* are you!" he snarls at the man, but even as he is speaking these words, his perception of the man changes. The man is somehow, somewhat misshapen, crooked, but his chest is deep, strong, and he clearly has no fear of Twomey, no emotion whatsoever shows in his face, only a mean determination as he moves closer repeating Twomey's question, turning it back on him, shifting the emphasis, "Who the fuck are *you*!" his voice a tense, dangerous whisper. His hands are reaching. Twomey looks frantically to see if he is armed. A scream for help strangles in his throat as he wakes in terror that such an odd unknown face and crooked body could find its way into his dream.

Beside him in the dark Jenny snores lightly, the sheet flared up over her hip. The room is as it has always been. The door is shut, and it occurs to him that in the dream he has heard the exact sound of that doorknob turning, the little rusty squeak it always makes being turned. He considers the fact that often a dream crystallizes around a sound—the ringing of a clock, the drip of water. It seems unlikely that he would have dreamed the sound of that doorknob. As he attempts to think back on the dream, it seems to him that the sound of the doorknob was the beginning of the dream, and it seems entirely possible to him then that someone did in fact turn the doorknob and that the sound was the impetus for the dream. It might simply have been one of the boys. Perhaps Larry came home late from Washington and wanted to look in to say hello, saw them sleeping, went to bed. Or perhaps Jimbo wanted to ask something and looked in to see if they were awake.

Other vague half-memories stir in his mind, and he recalls again that strange pocked face in the dream, the crooked body, the camouflage clothes (what could they indicate? something, someone hidden away?) A cold sweat chills his back. The newspapers are full of terrifying accounts of intruders, whole families murdered in their sleep. A shadow might be stepping down the hall to the boys' rooms right now, knife in his hand. *Nonsense. No. You know it's nothing.*

You have to get up and look. You're a coward if you put your head down again.

He reaches carefully to the nightstand for his watch, presses the illumination button on it. Five-thirty. Soon time to get up anyway.

He rises quietly, steps into his slippers, kneels and peers beneath the bed, moves to the closet, steps in and shuts the door after him not to wake Jenny, and in the moment before he pulls the string to light the overhead bulb in the closet, it occurs to him that a figure could be standing there immediately in front of him, the man with the pocked face. Or standing behind the clothes hangers. Even as he pulls the string, he feels it could release a flood of light to reveal a pocked, staring face, not inches from his own.

The string clicks. Light comes on. Nothing. Of course. Feel behind the hangers to be certain. Nothing. Of course. From the shelf he lifts down the five-cell flashlight and makes his way through the house, looks into Jimbo's room to see the boy sleeping neatly on his back, hands above the covers as if on display, Larry's room —he is back— his suitcase open on the floor, dirty clothes strewn out of it. Larry sleeps with the covers bunched between his legs, face thrown back, mouth open in a vague smile.

Nothing in the bathroom, of course. Nothing in the linen closet, nothing in the alcove beneath the stairs, nothing in the kitchen, the pantry, the hall closet, the guest bathroom, beneath the cellar stairs, in the furnace room, the laundry room, nothing. All the while he does this he knows with growing certainty that nothing is here yet feels compelled to conduct this ritual to master the fear still clinging to his spine at the lingering image of that pocked face of a stranger who entered his dream and challenged him: *Who the fuck are you?*

When he has looked everywhere, he thinks for one moment about the fact that a person hiding in the house could conceivably have slipped from one hiding place to another, from a place he has not yet checked to one he already has, but he immediately dismisses this. A reassuring ritual is one thing; that would be compulsion, obsession. No.

In the living room, he stands staring out at the lawn, quiet and still in the darkness. Disappointment touches him that it has stopped snowing, that only a very thin layer spots the lawn. He looks at the magnolia, the apple trees, trying to remember something that has escaped him. *The children in the apple tree,* he thinks. *Not known because not looked for. But heard, half-heard, in the stillness between two waves of the sea.* Words again. Words words words. His eyes lift to the dark sky. No stars. But off to the left a bright slash of moonlight against an edge of silver cloud. Overcast. It might snow again today, he thinks hopefully.

It is nearly quarter to six. He decides to make coffee, get breakfast ready now. But first he returns quietly to the bedroom, slips in without turning on the light and feels on the bureau top for his ring, holds it in his fingers for a moment, feeling the smooth gold circle as he does everyday, thinks about it, what it means. Sometimes when he forgets what his life is about, when his mind drifts or when he gets black-eyed, impatient, when he looks at Jenny and sees a stranger, when he just wants to go, get away, sometimes he can just touch the ring on his finger and feel calm again. He slips it on, breathes deeply, slowly.

It occurs to him as he lays the breakfast table, moving through a familiar stream of small acts—placing cups, bowls, spoons, sugar on the table, filling the coffee machine, lifting boxes and canisters from cupboard shelves—that this morning ritual he has followed for the past many years, nearly twenty, is a cherished segment of his life. Here in the warm kitchen, surrounded by familiar objects that he arranges in a fixed way to prepare for the appearance of his wife and children, he knows the quietness of a profound satisfaction, the practising of a normal existence, to have been allowed to experience the love of children, to have managed a life that is not a disaster, to have survived youth, his youth, those years that nearly undid him. Broken images of those years begin to surface in his mind, the desert, Katey, the...*no*. He turns from it, concentrates on the movements of his hands, the band of gold shining on his finger.

He screws off the top of a jar of vitamin pills and places one beside each of the four juice glasses on the table. The agreeably bitter aroma of vitamin B brings to mind the smell of the drug store where he had an afternoon job in high school, delivering prescriptions: that smell was the smell of vitamin B he found out by asking Emil Best, the proprietor.

"What's that smell, Mr. Best?"

"That's vitamin B, Fred."

*Ask and you shall be told.* Four hours twice a week, buck an hour plus tips. Nothing really. Little cash in the pocket. But that wasn't the point. That job was another ritual that gave meaning to his life, although it would be years, decades, before he would understand that. First, along with much of the rest of his generation, he had to attempt to destroy convention and tradition, only to learn that what lay beneath it all is a chaos too dangerous to confront—a chaos from which we protect ourselves by ritual and measure. Something you can not know except by faith or by teaching yourself, and the lesson is an arduous one.

He held the vitamin jar beneath his nose a moment, inhaling the aroma, before recapping it. It pleased him that his children had never questioned that they were required to swallow a vitamin pill each morning. It pleased him to think of all the nutritious food he and Jenny had provided for them over the years, how they had happily consumed it. When he was a boy, he had two peanut butter and jelly sandwiches on Wonder Bread for lunch everyday provided with the best of intentions by his mother. Twomey gobbled them down happily each day, but he couldn't help but think that healthier lunches might have saved him a good deal of trouble with his teeth. His mother never thought of the fact that it was junk to feed a kid. She didn't realize, as Twomey had discovered, that kids are just as happy to eat tomatoes and lettuce and cucumbers on slices of unbleached full grain bread.

He thinks of Jimbo who has turned vegetarian of late, won't even eat eggs or chicken ("Have you ever seen the conditions those chickens live under?" "Well, you're right, of course, but still...") Twomey cautions himself to let the boy have his convictions, warns himself to resist that urge he senses within himself to slap the boy down, wonders if that is universal, the other side of Oedipus. It seems odd to him that he only feels this antagonism for Jimbo, whose convictions are all toward what might be thought of as "the good" (though Twomey had his reservations about that), whereas Larry, who is into heavy metal and general hedonism, in no way irritates him.

They saw an item in the paper a while back about the member of a rock group called Deth Metal who committed suicide, leaving a note that complained the world was not evil enough for him. He blew his brains out, and the other members of the group found him and were reported to have gathered up the skull fragments and sold them to his fans to wear as jewelry. Larry's reaction to this was laughter while Jimbo was irate, and somehow Twomey found himself siding with Larry, even despite all the potentially painful associations involved (maybe *because* of them) and the bizarre twist of his arguing with Jimbo, of all people, his dead brother's namesake, about it. Still, he believed, wished to believe, that Jimbo was now among his pantheon of ancestors, one of the clear-eyed portrait photos in his workroom, beyond the painful realm of life. He felt that they were capable of advising him, Jimbo, too, even if his life had been flawed, like the lives of the gods themselves. Of course, he didn't for a moment really *believe* any of this. But still...

"Son, one of the things you learn with the years," he said to Jimbo, "is that you don't know nearly as much as you thought you did when you started out—that you *can't*. All the stuff that can seem so logical to you, so evidently *right* is, well, can show itself to be, well, not *feasible*. On the other hand, you also learn that most of the others don't know either—that if you fear your own ignorance and try to be perfect and exact you'll never get anything done."

"That just sounds like a lot of cynicism to me." This from Jimbo's pale face, mouth small with inner torment that broke Twomey's heart. "You have to recognize, Dad, that your values are not necessarily mine."

"Point taken." Twomey was amazed. Had he himself ever had the gumption to say such a thing to his own father?

As the tea steeps on the kitchen table, Nicola mews around his legs, making small speak noises at him, as though she is trying to imitate human speech. Twomey breaks out a can of Whiskas, pops the top and forks it into a bowl, trying not to smell it, puts it on the floor and the cat rubs the side of her face against his wrist as she bows her head to the food. Twomey watches her sleek haunches, the black fur glistening like silver, white paws. He had never liked cats, but Nicola wore him down. She picked them a year ago, started visiting them late last summer, appearing at odd moments to brush up against their legs or sit on the lawn watching them with an interest that little by little loosened their resistance to allowing her into their lives.

It turned out she was owned by one of Larry's classmates in sophomore year, a girl who lived two streets over. The reason Nicola had run from them was because their other cat, Nicola's own male offspring, a larger, stronger animal, was bullying her, driving her away from the food, biting her, scratching. When Jenny told the girl's mother that the cat wanted to move in here, they tried to take it back at first, but the cat wouldn't stay, so finally they let it go. The other cat, the male, was called Victor, and even now, when Nicola had been with them for nearly two years, Victor would show up from time to time, try to get in, try to drive Nicola away. Weird, he thinks. Her own offspring.

The way it is with animals. Some people, too, no doubt.

On the ledge beside the frosted kitchen window he notices a book, a dogeared paperback, which he glances idly at, waiting for the tea. *Where Are the Children?* A book he's never read, doesn't even remember owning. Maybe Jenny's. He remembers that he meant to ask Jenny about it. She sometimes picks up a used thriller from the second-hand shop to read herself to sleep. He knew this book, knew the author slightly. She'd been in one of his workshops when he was a student. Surprise of the term was when she came in with a photocopy of a million dollar check. Paperback advance. You could've choked to death on the envy in that room. Wonder did the money do her good?

The cat is at his leg again just as he is about to remove the leaves from the tea, looking up at him with her little speech noises. Wants to go out. He opens the back door for her, watches her pause alertly on the threshold, peer out for potential danger. Seem strange if a person did that, but perfectly natural for a cat. See me hunched inside the front door, looking right and left for the pock-faced man like Nicola keeps alert for Victor.

Strange.

Never liked cats, told them they could keep her but don't expect me to do a damn thing for her, and now of course it's me who feeds her every morning. Don't mind. Fits right into my ritual. Another reason for it all. Depends on me.

The cat leaps out into the dark morning and Twomey bumps the back door shut, feels the icy draft across his slippered feet, thinks for some reason of his mother in the kitchen of his boyhood, in her kitchen now, alone, don't think of this, his father dead from drink, his sister from cancer, his brother by his own hand as they say. How can you grow so far from people you once loved so fiercely? Your ancestors. You think of your mother as though she's already dead, how can you? All the things that never could be reconciled. Who was it? Wilde: *We start out loving our parents, then we judge them, few if any ever forgive them.* Something like that. Forgive them for what? And who am I to judge? Judge not that you be not. They gave a lot. Lot they didn't give, too. Lot they couldn't. Some they wouldn't. And now

69

see the little breaches begin to gather with your own already. Thought your own love for your two darlings was supernatural. You've already sullied it. Just a little, but it will no doubt get worse.

Way of life. Don't expect the impossible. Still, if you bring life into the world, you ought to do your best, follow through all the way. We're only human, but a serious man has to expect certain things of himself. Are you serious? Perhaps.

Then he remembers something from long ago that he does not wish to think about and which brings the blood into his cheeks. He finds another thought to move to, his father's love for him, that it was more reticent than his for his own two sons. Or was it just harder for him to express it? Did he go round with a heart full of pain? Unable to release his feeling?

Trash. He could have addressed me. Asked questions. What do you think about that, son? What are your views on this? What do you hope for? No. He was tired out and nothing put aside for me. Left just enough for mother to survive on. Not a penny more. Had to take care of myself. And what did he leave behind, one son who shot himself in the head, another who can't stand to visit his own mother—no, no, not true exactly, there are reasons, extenuating circumstances...

He lifts the filter out of the teapot, pours a mug, covers the pot with a cozy, carries the cup up to the bedroom, sets it on the night table and sits on the edge of the bed. He can feel the warmth of Jenny's body radiating from beneath the covers. He lays his palm on her warm soft cheek, thinks perhaps if he could make love to her now, right now, his troubled mind would go calm. His face moves closer to hers, but she grunts, he sees a warning wrinkle at the edge of her nose. In two, three seconds she will explode. He rises, whispers, "Cup of tea here, Jenny," back down to the kitchen. She needs time with the demons she must confront on the perimeters between sleep and waking. In fifteen, twenty minutes, she will be transformed and radiant while his day will already have begun to sink slowly downward.

He taps at Larry's and Jimbo's doors and is already seated at the breakfast table drinking coffee and not looking at the *Times* folded in half on the table before him when Larry appears, grabbing for yogurt and cornflakes before he even sits.

"How was Washington?"

"It was freaking *great!*" he says, pouring cornflakes and yoghurt simultaneously from either hand, a heavy-built round-faced boy with a space between his front teeth.

*"Freaking,"* Jimbo repeats with a smirk, coming in after him.

"Hey!" Larry says, turning sharply in his chair and leaning forward menacingly. "Get off my back! Or I'll attack! And you don't want that!"

For a moment Twomey is startled by the ferocity of the boy before he realizes he's joking, mouthing some rap lyric. He watches Jimbo to see if he registers fear, but nothing shows on the older, taller boy's face or in his posture. He sits, takes yoghurt. Twomey notes he's wearing a tee shirt that says *Euro Holidays Are Not My Holidays.*

Now Jenny is coming through the door, too, almost herself already, and Twomey can't help but peek at the alluring flesh between the slightly parted lapels of her ivory white satin pajamas. *"Boys,"* she warns.

Larry blinks and smiles at her in a sugary parody of being adorable. "Yes, mother?"

"You're not turning swishy on us are you, Lar?" Twomey asks.

"Fred!"

Jimbo says, "Dad, could you drop the sexist slurs."

"PC stooge," says Larry.

"Aw, can't you take a joke?" Twomey asks, still annoyed despite himself by the tee shirt, realizing that his comment was gauged to annoy not Larry but Jimbo and feeling like a stooge himself to his own emotions.

"You think it's funny to laugh at minority groups? You must have a pretty weak self image."

"You're right, of course, son. I apologize."

"Yeah," says Larry. "Dad's sorry. He didn't realize you're a nancy boy."

"I'm *not* a nancy boy!" He slaps his palm flat on the table so the cups rattle in their saucers. "I just don't think it's humorous to mock people because they're different! That's what's wrong with this fucking lousy world! Everyone wants to feel big by kicking somebody weaker!"

"Language, Jimbo," says Larry, so perfectly seriously that Twomey can barely overpower his urge to laugh, but he says, "Hey, take it easy now everybody. Jimbo is right. I was out of line, and I apologize, but I really did not mean it seriously."

"Maybe that's the problem, Dad," Jimbo says. "Maybe you should get serious."

"Oh, hang it on your fucking ear," says Larry, and Jenny explodes: "That's it! You all shut up *now* or I'm gone!"

Everyone shuts up. Her explosions, rare as they are, are effective, which Twomey secretly resents. Is she stronger than me? Am I a wimp? He feels lousy now, as though the day is already poisoned and getting worse, his relationship with his son a little more tainted for no reason. How could I do that? Act like a fool. Antagonize my own son. He thinks how sweet the boy was as a child, how caring, feels his life gone wrong, dismisses the thought as over-reaction, but is powerless to lighten the mood he himself has invited to bloom in him.

Moments pass in which the silence is framed by the scrape of cup on saucer, the click of spoon against bowl, the sizzle of coffee pouring from the pot.

Larry rises. "Okay if I put the radio on?"

Twomey looks to Jenny. "Sure," he says. She is now buried in the *Times*. Twomey feels the day begin to heal as a chorus of women on the radio sing, "Why can't you be like Elvis? Why can't you sing like El-elvis?" He pours more coffee into his cup, milk, feels his mind relax and begin to turn to the class he will teach today.

Jenny looks up from her paper. "You only have one class today."

"Right."

"Know what you're going to do today after your class?"

He knows from the look in her eyes, what she will say because they know one another so well after all these years, all sorts of invisible signals they could read and sometimes misread, and he is annoyed but plays straight man, hoping that he has misread, that she will say something other than what she says.

"Go to your mother's. To invite her for Christmas dinner."

"I was going to call..."

"You have to *go* there, Fred. You haven't been there since we got back from Canton."

"I think I was."

"You weren't."

"I call her. Every week almost. Almost always."

"Fred: You have to *go* there."

The boys are now pulling on jackets, slinging on knapsacks, saying their goodbyes for the day. It occurs to Twomey that they enjoy seeing their father on the defensive, exposed. Jenny is right, of course; he dreads going to see his mother, but he knows Jenny is right, knows that he was putting it off as long as he could, knowing that sooner or later she would challenge him, force him to face it.

The side door slams. He can hear footsteps in the alley, the sound of the garage door lifting on its pulley. Something teases at his mind, half-remembered for an instant then gone. What? *Where Are the Children?* As he turns to ask his wife about it, he hears the gears of Larry's mountain bike clicking off down the alley, then the sound of a key in the side door, and Jimbo is back.

"My bike's flat."

"Probably a slow leak," Twomey says. "Come on, let's see if we can pump it up." He knows his son is perfectly capable of doing this himself, but welcomes the opportunity to smooth things over. The morning air, light now, steel grey in the sky, penetrates his pajamas and robe instantly, and he hurries to the garage, savoring its wonderfully sour aroma of mildew and old varnish, rubbing his hands together to warm them. He goes to take the pump from his own bike, notices that his is flat, too, but for some reason he does not understand, he chooses not to mention it.

He unscrews the valve cap from his son's rear wheel, fits the pump valve onto the tube and begins to pump. It pleases him that his arms are strong enough to pump easily, experiences a boyish pride at being able to show off this way in front of his son as his left hand, holding the tire, feels the rubber fill and tighten. When he removes the pump, the air holds in the tire. He checks the front wheel—it's tight. He bounces the rear wheel a couple of times, checks it again. It's still tight and full.

"You're fine," he says."

"Thanks, Dad," Jimbo says and hugs him, something he does rarely these days. Twomey holds the boy to him, slaps his back manfully. "Have a nice day, buddy," he says, hearing the lameness of the cliché in his own ears yet at the same time braced by the emotion behind it. He watches Jimbo peddle off down the alley before turning to his own bike. Both tires are flat. He pumps them up, bounces them. Fine. Shakes his head as he fits the pump back to his crossbar, wondering about the fact that Larry's bike was okay. Larry has the only mountain bike, while both Twomey and Jimbo have three-speed Raleighs.

He decides not to mention it to Jenny who, for all her lightness of heart, can be susceptible to severe fits of paranoia over such things. Twomey can, too, but he is capable of ignoring it while she gets sucked right in.

Yet despite his decision, as soon as he is back inside, standing in the door, watching his wife at the breakfast table read the world's horror stories of the day about ethnic cleansing in the Balkans and the variety of American and other murders here, there, and everywhere, he hears himself say, "Mine was flat, too. Both wheels. Pumped 'em up good as new, though."

"That's weird," she says, just as he knew she would. *Why did he tell her, then?* "I see unhealthy connections beginning to turn in the wheels of your eyes," he says. *Maybe just to be able to make her experience the paranoia so he could tell her it was nonsense.* "Paranoia city."

"Well how could that happen? *Two* flats? *Two* bikes? Do you think somebody is doing this?"

"Why do you use progressive tense? It happened once, and there's probably some logical explanation for it."

"Like what?"

"Like for example the weather. It was way below freezing last night and now it's just above. That could affect rubber, or air pres-

74

sure."

"Was Larry's flat, too?"

"He's got special tires. Mountain bike, remember?"

She gives him a skeptical look, but he can see she is grudgingly accepting his faux naturalistic explanation. He kisses her forehead. "I better get ready."

"Are you going straight from school to your mother's?"

"You are relentless."

Upstairs, on the way to the bathroom, he stops at the door to Jimbo's room, turns the knob and shoves the door open. On the wall is a Greenpeace poster of a rubber speedboat buzzing a whaler at whose stern a harpoonist is aiming for a blue whale glistening in the sunlight. On another wall an Indian shaman dances like a tilted pinwheel in black and white, on a third a majestic picture of a Bengal tiger over the caption, *Tyger tyger fading out...*

What reasonable person could argue with any of it, he asks himself, remembering all the arguments *he* had with people in the sixties. In his neighborhood they used to call him Fred X because he refused to allow people to say the word *Nigger* in his presence; he would correct them, "Negro." Then it got to be a joke so if he said the word "Negro," *they* would correct *him*, say, "Nigger," and he was forced in that way to drop the whole thing. It occurs to him now that for all their received bigotry, they were good-natured about it. They actually allowed him to be who he was more good-naturedly than he treated them. He disdained their narrow-mindedness, yet in some way they seemed to wear their bigotry casually, calmly as a man might wear his parents' bias for ham over beef. He does not understand what lies at the bottom of these thoughts, and they worry him slightly, make him wonder whether he has by now sold himself so far down the river that he is actually trying to find excuses for the existence of bigotry.

He hears Jimbo's voice, calm and reasonable in his ear: "Don't you understand, Dad, that your values are not necessarily mine?"

"Don't *you* understand that *my* values are not necessarily mine?"

75

"I don't understand what you mean by that. It sounds like a meaningless paradox to me. A cop out."

"It was a joke, son. You know? Joke? A thing to make people laugh and feel good."

"What's funny about bigotry?"

"Jimbo, lighten up. I am not your enemy. You know, like life is a bitch and then you die. Try to enjoy yourself a little. And others."

"How? By eating eggs laid by chickens that live in the most extreme misery imaginable? By..."

Oh Jimbo boy, I remember when you were a lad. You were so sweet, you taught me the meaning of love, I never would have thought things would take this turn, what can I do to make it right again? I'm not going to take on responsibility for the world and all the creatures in it. If there are only 5,000 tigers left in the world that is extremely unfortunate and I salute you for trying to help the fund to save them, but honestly, Jim, I've got other concerns. I'm sorry. I've only got another twenty-five years, maybe thirty, left, maybe a little more, maybe less, maybe much less, and I want to enjoy what I got as best I can.

Mounted on the wall above the boy's desk is a hunting knife in a leather sheath, a knife Twomey had given him as a gift on his fifteenth birthday, a gag, with a note, "To help cut through the bullshit of this world." Now Twomey finds himself wondering would it hurt a lot going in. He shakes the thought, shakes free of some unpleasant thought about Jimbo trying to find its way into his consciousness, shakes away from a recurring fragment of the dream that woke him nearly three hours before, pictures that pock-faced man reaching up to the wall for this knife — no.

"*Them old dreams are only in your head,*" he whispers and goes in to wash his face, managing not to think, not quite to think the words painted on a mailbox in the little room alongside his consciousness.

# Chapter Six

Twomey sits on the edge of the desk and looks from face to face in the room—from JoAnne Iacono the cute little Italian girl who always calls him "Professor" at one end, and over to Eric Slovak the rock-jawed football player who surprisingly has the most refined critical sense in the room. With the exception of one or two, they are all about the age he was when his father died, but most of them seem to him in better shape than he was, mentally, emotionally. Though he sometimes thinks wistfully of fumbled opportunities from his youth (a girl named Claire who liked him, a crack at Brown, a job at Columbia), he in no way envies the years of learning and confusion and painful experience these young people have ahead of them. He gazes for a moment at Eloise Cremp, a slender girl who is almost pretty despite the acne, but in whose close-set grey eyes he feels he sees the edge of insuperable depression. We're all alone, he thinks, but somehow a person like that believes she is the only one there, locked in that room, and her response to the impenetrability of the walls is to sink down into a hole so deep and black she loses all sense of up and down, all sense of depth. He knew a girl once, years before, who suffered like that. Katey. Her face appears in his mind now, so pretty, so fragile, and he feels a terrible remorse about to open inside him remembering how he abandoned her, knowing there is no other word for it; he turns his thoughts from the word, from her, from those years, glances from the intense Indian head nickel face of Joseph Draper in the middle row, the cherubic tanned beachboy face of Alan Serafino (that name's *got* to be an alias), his thoughts flickering quickly from the memory of seeing Serafino in the dorm hall as he hotfooted away from Janet Fallow's room, to the vaguely comical expression of bewilderment on Walter Gatzy whose mouth smiles and eyes seem in constant fear that the joke is on him, to Xavier Green, an older boy, mid-twenties maybe, whose face at once attracts and repulses him. Green was also in Montpelier at the Convention. He is an intense student who Twomey has an idea never finished high school. Equivalency test maybe. Maybe in prison. He has that pallor, those eyes he'd seen on a couple of guys he knew who went to jail in the sixties and come out with different faces—at once alert, obedient, scornful, knowing things about humanity that most people couldn't even imagine. Green knew more or less what he had to know and worked hard, but his perceptions were always just slightly off. Twomey feels pity for the boy, but wishes he would go away.

Twomey picks his victim.

"Mr. Gatszy: What is reality?"

Gatszy says, "Reality." That smile, those eyes. "Is what is...*real.*" With great conviction. Not a clue.

"Such as?"

"This desk. Me. The sun."

Twomey nods thoughtfully, glances out the window, "Kind of grey sun today," hears the chuckles, turns his glance to others.

"The real things," Bernard Minex says through his protruding teeth. "The things that really matter."

"Like?"

"What you read in the newspaper as opposed to what you read in a novel," says Eric Slovak, watching him cautiously. Kid's got the world by the balls, smart, good-looking, athlete with sensitivity.

Twomey reaches behind him on the desk, produces a tabloid. "Here is a newspaper." He reads the headline: *Duck-billed Baby Found in Henhouse.* Reality?"

"That's the damn *National Enquirer,*" says Slovak. "I was thinking more like *the New York Times. The Washington Post.*"

"So you don't consider this report of the duck-billed baby found in a henhouse as part of reality? What about this?" He reaches back for a Picasso print. *Girl at the Mirror.* "Reality?"

"*Sur*reality," Gatszy blurts, and JoAnne Iacona turns her cute brown face and says, "It's *cubism*, dolt."

"But is it reality, Ms. Iacono," Twomey asks, looking into her brown eyes and thinking to himself, If I were Eric Slovak, who I surmise you are warm for, I would crap-pail this class and go make love to you, Ms Iacono, very thoroughly.

She thinks hard, a cagey Sicilian who will not be forced into a blunder and very well-read behind her New York gruff accent. "If you mean like is that picture itself, that print you're holding *real, yeah*."

"*Excellent*," says Twomey and feels love well up in his heart as he always does when a student tunes in. He sees such pleasure in Ms. Iacona's brown eyes that his heart goes out to her; she should have more praise and attention.

"So you are distinguishing a work of art as object from a work of art as form and content. The style of the Picasso is cubist, right? And the picture might be said to attempt to *deal* with reality by showing us many different angles at once. In other words, by giving us *more* of reality, the artist destroys the *illusion* that what he is painting is real. Remember, perspective is a deception, right? It makes you think you are seeing distance when in fact what you are looking at is a flat surface. So instead, Picasso gives us here another, more embracing piece of reality, flat and many-angled. Yet it is only a fragment of actual reality which, as Mr. Gatszy rightly pointed out, is *everything*. You, me, the sun, the grey sky, and everything under, above, behind, and in front of it."

Gatszy is beaming. Cherub-faced Alan Serafino sits forward in his chair, eyes wide and blue as the sky, says softly, "Wow!"

Twomey takes another print from the little stack on his desk, Magritte's super-realistic painting of a pipe, captioned, *Ceci n'est pas un pipe*. "What about this?" he asks. "Any French speakers here? What's it say?"

"This is not a pipe," volunteers Joanne Iacono.

"Is *not* a pipe?" asks Gatzy. "Or *is* a pipe?"

"Is *not*," Twomey tells him.

"But it *is* a pipe," Gatzy persists, making Twomey want to kiss him in gratitude for stepping right into it. "Is it?"

Incredulous, Gatzy insists, "Yes, it is. What is this, like a terminology trick or something? If it's not a pipe, what is it, then? A snorkel in disguise?"

Joanne Iacono smirks. "Funny guy."

Twomey tries not to imagine her naked. "It's a picture. It's paper and pigments."

Now Gatzy is impatient. "Yeah, but it's a picture of a pipe, so it is a pipe."

Poor bastard. "Like to try smoking it?" Clearly Gatszy still has not quite grasped it, thinks Twomey a boring pedant.

"Tell me," Twomey says and cruises his eyes around the room again. "What is realism?"

"Depicting what is real," Slovak says fast, too fast—he forgot to think; he knows better.

"Let me ask you to apply that to *The Floating Opera* by John Barth," Twomey says, and out of the corner of his eye sees Gene Kelty, who apparently despises Twomey, shove his finger down his throat. Without looking at him, Twomey says, "That's Barth not barf, Mr. Kelty," saving the moment for himself turning the joke on Kelty, whose pale Scot face goes beet red, but Twomey knows he will be no more trouble the rest of the day; he's had his shot and blown it.

"In the beginning of the novel we are told, 'I never wrote a novel before but I have read a few to try to get the hang of it…' What is the function of that statement?"

"Honesty," pronounces Gatzy with sincere conviction. "It establishes the credibility of the character."

JoAnne Iacona says, "Does it have to do with the fact that it's Barth's first novel?"

"In fact," says Twomey," pouncing, "Barth wrote a couple of novels before that one which were never published. So he is *lying* if he is telling us *he* never wrote a novel before."

"But it's fiction, right?" says Slovak, and Twomey pounces in his direction, "Yes! Precisely. It is fiction. It is a novel and the main character, the narrator, is addressing the reader directly as though *he* is writing the novel himself, right before our eyes. How can a fictional character address the reader?" He holds up the Magritte again. "Can this pipe be smoked?" And the Picasso again. "Can this cubistic woman here speak to us?"

They chuckle. "Not likely," says JoAnne Iacono, experiencing the difference between a human being and an image in paint or words.

"Right! No! It is an illusion. It is, in fact, more than that. It is anti-illusion! And it is rendered in a *realistic* style!"

He sees the clouds of consternation on each face he looks at. Good. Now for the sunlight.

"In other words, realism is not reality, but an illusion of reality. Barth is writing a novel, and he pretends he is speaking directly to us and because of that we *believe* him. He creates an illusion and *seems* to destroy the illusion. This is a novel I am writing, he tells us, the first one I've ever written, and we *believe* him. This guy is telling us straight from the shoulder, I never did this before. *No!* He is *lying!* Anti-illusion. And we are caught in the trap! He's a magician pulling a rabbit out of a hat. It's just a trick, but we *believe* it!"

He sees the delight of comprehension taking hold of face after face in the room, and the appearance fills his heart with love. "We're talking about metafiction here, peoples. Heady stuff. Listen to this. Ever hear of Alain Robbe Grillet? Well about forty years ago he said this, 'Academic criticism in the west, as in communist countries, employs the word 'realism' as if reality were already entirely consti-tuted when the writer comes on the scene. Thus it supposes that the latter's role is limited to *explaining* and *expressing* the reality of his period'—instead of *creating* it." He pauses to let it sink in.

"In other words, we have the idea here that possibly, just possibly, reality is not fixed, that our *perception* of reality is not fixed, that real-ity, or the piece of reality we are able to deal with at any given moment or to which we are privy via our necessarily limited point of view is a kind of fiction that we created in order to be able in some measure to have the illusion of understanding our lives and negotiating the world. In other words, you, me, and the sun, Mr. Gatszy, are in a sense, a *fiction*. The fiction of our perceptions of these things just as in the beginning of Barth's second novel, *End of the Road*, the narrator begins by saying, 'In a sense I am Jacob Horner...' In a sense, Ms. Iacona, I *am* Frederic Twomey!"

How he loves his life at this moment, staring into the brown eyes of JoAnne Iacono who has received a new thought from him and is admiring it.

Xavier Green has his index finger up in the air. Twomey gives him the floor with a nod. Green says, "But these books you're talkin' about, I haven't read 'em, I admit, but like. It's written with the 'I', like, voice, right? So it *is* the author. The author is writing the words, the author is saying, 'I'."

"You haven't read the books, Mr. Green."

"I haven't read the books, Professor Twomey."

"Read the books, Mr. Green..."

"Yeah, but, it's like a mirror, right? Like a mirror of life." He looks so pleased to have fished that phrase out of his word pool that Twomey hates to take the pleasure from him, but says, "Fiction is not a mirror. It's a hammer."

He sees incomprehension on several faces. "Which means?" He zeros in. "Ms Iacono?" Chance for greatness. She hesitates. Serafino says, "To destroy." Flicker of something I don't like in those blue eyes. Twomey tilts his head with reservation. "Or...?"

Iacono blurts, "To build?"

Twomey smiles slowly. "Think about it." The bell rings. "Mr. Green," he says, "read the books and then we can discuss it in conference."

In the hall outside, Geoffrey Burns is standing alongside the fire extinguisher mounted on the wall. Twomey can see he's waiting for him, thinks, *Shit,* but accepts the suggestion that they have a cup of coffee in Burns's office; he has no real choice, even though he doesn't really have time.

He glances at his watch as he says, "Sure," and Burns catches it. "Got an appointment?"

Twomey sighs. "Yeah. I promised Jenny I'd go see my mother today."

"That bad?"

Burns's tone is friendly, conciliatory maybe. Let's put it behind us, forget what happened. But still, Twomey thinks, he's got something he can use if it ever suits him. Twomey shrugs, sighs again, says, "Bad enough," and feels like a shit: It's your *mother*, man. Your *mother*.

Burns has a better office than Twomey, a corner office with a tall, segmented window in each wall of the right angle. It is well-appointed, too, neat, with a well-stocked bar concealed behind the locked cabinet in the shelves, in comparison to the bottle of Jim Beam in the bin-drawer of Twomey's metal desk. The walls are adorned with two groupings of framed prints, one a set of Goya reproductions—demons paring their nails, a sleeping man dreaming of monsters; the other an original series of prints by an artist named Gladys Swan called *Voices from the Volcano*—sky formations, twisted birds above a black and white volcano. The room is inviting, comfortable, not so neat that it would put you on edge, even its little bits of disorder seem like displays—a ragged-edged bundle of manuscripts tied with a ribbon, a not-quite even stack of books.

In a number of ways, Twomey admires, even envies Burns a little. They are the same age, and Burns is good-looking with an athlete's grace and more successful as a writer than Twomey, although Twomey suspects his own stories are more complex, his range greater, and figures everyone probably more or less thinks that about himself in comparison to his colleagues. Up until now, Burns has been one of his best friends here, and he almost feels good sitting in his office, though he cannot help but wonder whether he himself, had he not wasted more than ten years of his life before finishing his education and getting serious, might have done better, gone further, written more, got a better foothold.

Burns pours coffee into two white porcelain mugs — no styrofoam here, while Twomey makes small talk waiting for Burns to get to the point. It would be rude to rush it, say, *So what's up, Geoff? You still pissed off about Janet? Nothing actually happened, you know.* Another opening occurs to him. "Jenny tells me you came by the other day?"

Burns's eyes are startled. Yeah, Twomey thinks, Jenny tells me things, we communicate, so don't think you can play mind games with her or me or us about something that never even really happened. "She said you wanted to see me."

"Oh, that's right, I did come by. Wanted to ask you something."

"Shoot."

Burns's smile is faint. "Do me a favor, will you Fred?"

Twomey's thigh tenses. *What now?* "What?"

"I need a letter of recommendation."

"You moving on?"

"No. Susan and I may go the adoption route."

Twomey notices suddenly how old he looks, the grey in his moustache. He thinks how it would be to suddenly become the father of an infant again now, one that is not even your own, wonders about it, thinking of all the years since his two were born, of his current sadness over Jimbo. Foolish. The boy is just going through the end of his adolescence. Not nearly as bad as you yourself had it.

"We've got one last try at making our own baby," Burns says and sips his coffee. He tips back in his chair and looks up at the wall where the dustjacket of his first book hangs in a frame. "We'd use an egg from a donor. Our clinic is IFF-America which is a subsidiary of IFF-Australia. Ever hear of them?"

Twomey shakes his head.

"ABC did an exposé of the parent company. They seem professional enough, but we've had conflicts on things. Like whether or not we get a say about the donor."

"If they're jerking you around, why not go somewhere else?"

Burns warms his palms around the white mug, holding it close against the center of his chest. "Can't. The insurance company decides who we use." He looks into Twomey's face again. "Meanwhile I'm giving Susan progesterone shots every night, and I hate every minute of it. They use this oily base that requires large gauge needles so she spouts gore every time. Maybe it's my fault. Clumsy."

"How's your father doing?" Twomey asks because he can think of nothing else to say and fears he might let out some unprocessed thoughts that will be less than helpful to his friend's frame of mind.

Burns merely stares at him with his grey eyes. Twomey thinks of the eyes of a character in an Ambrose Pierce story, a confederate soldier being hanged, the grey eyes of a sniper.

"The debate is still going on in my family. Whether to terminate his life by cutting off his nutrition. I always use the word 'kill' when we discuss it. I have doubts, of course. Who wouldn't? Either way. I went to see him last week. He stared at me. He looks like hell. I lied and said, You're looking good, and he raised one eyebrow - skeptically maybe—and made some guttural sounds. It's impossible to know whether he's still with us or not." He sips his coffee and falls silent while Twomey watches him, nothing available to say, wondering how to make his exit, grateful that Burns clearly has decided to gloss over the incidents at the NWP, that that little indiscretion is behind him.

Burns looks up again and asks, "Did you hear about the Golly killing?"

"Golly?"

"Yeah, saw it in the papers one day. Some teenaged kid whose last name is Golly. He's in his room listening to The Doors, to 'The End'—member that? Right. And he decides to kill his father. So he cranks the stereo up full blast and when his father comes in to yell at him, Golly opens fire with a semi-automatic weapon. Killed him dead. Then he killed a woman cop who showed up, and then he killed himself."

"Jesus Christ."

"Ain't easy being a dad, I guess."

"Or a son. Christ, you know, you couldn't write that? You couldn't write that as fiction. It's just not credible."

"Yeah," Burns says, glancing at him, "guess that's one way of looking at it."

## Shadow King

There are things working against you, inside yourself, at any given moment the breath and will might seep from you, leave you deflated as an empty sack, will-less.

You sit behind the wheel of the Chevy in the campus lot, notebook propped on the steering wheel, a blue plastic Bic between your fingers, as you work to find a vantage point in consciousness from which you can see. You write in the book, slowly, deliberately, glancing up from time to time across the snowy lot toward the faculty exit, watching.

Write, *To see*, watching the words on the page, and feel the hollow ache inside your skull, the emptiness that is your enemy, the chill beneath your leather jacket stronger than your will.

You want nothing now, feel nothing, desire nothing. You are nothing and all that you have against the emptiness is this thin thread of will to draw it upright, to propel it.

That morning you woke in your bed, curled up beneath the itching blanket, the wrinkled damp soiled sheet beneath your sweating body, and you could not get out of bed. You lay there and stared at the wall, heard the thumping feet of the people upstairs preparing for their day, heard the voice of the pregnant woman, the heavier steps of the man you saw the other day with the dark, lumpy face. Beyond the wall you heard voices arguing, no words, just tones of blurred anger, male, female, male, female, and the puckered plaster on the wall was a variety of odd faces watching you. Spirits there in the surface of the wall. Maybe you do not believe that, but why not? It could be. There could be dead souls everywhere staring at you, wanting something. What? That the price be paid. The current reversed.

This was a moment you knew from before in your life where there was no system, no one there to kick your bed, force you up, force you to play a role, to hide behind your silence, your blankness, your smile, your enthusiasm, fake it till you could get something, food, money, chances.

Now you have no one but yourself to drive you and if you run empty what is there? What could make you get up then? Who? You know this place, lay there and let minutes pass, an hour, a morning, a day. Crawl out of bed, eat whatever was there, plain bread, a slice of baloney, beans from a can, raw bacon. Put your mouth around the chalky water faucet and drink, crawl back in.

Or you watch tv, drink cheap tequila till you blur, till your mind vanishes into the grey of numbed sleep.

The faces in the wall watched you lie there in the pale light of morning, a woman with a pan-shaped face and flat eyes, imprisoned spirit, and a blade-faced man with two black glittering eyeballs trapped in the surface of the wall.

We will get you, we will suck you into the wall with us so all you can do is hang there and stare, flat-faced, at someone else on a bed who can't get up because the soul is eaten alive like a cockroach, black blood on the teeth of the white, empty, sucked-out morning.

Your mind felt soiled as the sheet you lay on. You tried to smooth it, search its surface, within its folds, for something to pull up on, out of this hole.

There was a word: DRAIOCHT. Magic in Irish, a word you had printed across the back of the apartment door, a word you could not pronounce and that gave it a special power. You stared at it sometimes to invite it into your body.

"Pretense," you whispered aloud as you lay there in bed, knowing you believed nothing of it, knowing yourself lost in a fat lie meant to fuel yourself with, ignite yourself like a sparkplug, but it was a lie, it was pretense.

You turned over in bed, peered through sagging lids across the room to the words printed on the door.

DRAIOCHT.

And beneath that:

MAGICK.

You drew the 'k' to your eye to taste its sweetness. 'K' for Kteis. Cunt. The magic of cunt was magick. You peered through the slit of your lids toward it but all you felt was the slack nothingness of pretense.

Your eyelids drooped lower, so all you saw was a slit of pale light that illuminated nothing, just a crescent of paleness, no malevolent demon, no guardian angel, only pathetic words inked on a door that you could no longer even see.

You are a lie. Your life is a lie. Beneath the bed, in the old boot box, nestled in wrapping paper was the Smith & Wesson .45, loaded. Bullets the size of your thumb could drive through the bonewall, plow across, forcing the soft brain out the rear skullwall, bone splinters, pulp, blood and finally, then, silence, forever, the end you should have had at his fucking hands all those years ago before you never even saw light. His decision. You shall have no voice, no eyes, no mind, you are not needed, you do not need to be, where your life would have been I draw an X.

You lie. Your life. A lie. Please. Die.

Upstairs, above the ceiling, the man's hammering steps crossed the floor, a door opened, a blurred voice spoke, the woman's feet, lighter sharper shorter steps, crossed the floor, the door slammed, four feet descended the stairway, echoing, and hatred seethed in your heart for their success in facing the day, a man and a pregnant woman together in a crummy apartment going out to a day together, to work, to have a life as if their lousy fucking life was worth anything at all in this pathetic place.

You remembered your mother out in the desert those years before you were taken from her, how she lay on the mattress in their shack, and you sat on the bare dusty floor eating a bowl of dry cereal, watching her. The image of her face came sharp now through the slit of your eyelids, and you could see her shallow eyes, her stillness that lay across the morning like the heavy blanket of the hot desert air, how she would lay there forever until one of the others came and shoved at her with a foot, forced her up to make food or to do what they did to her when they put the pillowcase over your head and tied it shut, laughing at you, once hanging you by the back of your belt to a hook in the lintel so you hung there kicking and swinging your arms and listening to their noises, grunting, snarls, shouts.

*Get up*, you thought, watching her through the slits of your lids, remembering on his tongue the dry taste of cornflakes. *Get up, please*, and the words found your lips where you yourself lay in the dirty chill bed all these years later. "*Get up!*" and your own body responded to the order, moved on the pinpoint force of will.

Your arms flung the blanket off, your body flung itself onto the dusty wood floor, stretched out, lowered to the wood, pushing up, counting as the movement burned into your blood, your chest, your triceps, as if you were two men, one driving the other with bitter, spiteful words, the other accepting abuse as a gift, like a fucking dog licking its master's boot.

Tears filmed your eyes, and the two men merged into a blurred image in your brain. You rested, panting, on your haunches, jaws clenched, then dropped forward again, counting aloud, hearing the desperate croak of the sounds of numbers formed by your throat, your mouth, grunted out on the jet of breath, up, down, counting...

*It is not pretense*, you write on the page of the notebook braced against the chill plastic steering wheel. Blow on your fingers to warm them with your breath. *The page of The Will is blank. You choose the truth to write there.*

He it is who is false. Double em. And he will pay for that. He will be made to see. He will be made to lose his advantage. I see his false manner. It is empty words. The cheating liar behind his words, his smiles.

Every false smile is a threat or a cringe. Existence as we know it is full of sorrow, a sentence of death. What do you experience when you smile? Why do you smile? What is really behind your smile? You know. You know. A smile is a tool, metal to be forged. A mask for a role. Know what you feel in your heart and conceal it, but know what you are doing. Until you are master of yourself you will be master of no one.

The bare white skull grins in its mask.

90

Consider his fear now, gestating like an egg, growing. Consider how to nourish it. To reverse the wave of evil. Turn it back on him, on the two nerd boys. My brothers. Ha. Let him turn on the spit of his fear. Teach him the life of fear he left to you. Leave him messages, teasing and hard to understand, let him try to know what it means, why, just as you did, wondering with the pillowcase tied over your head in the heat, and the man, the men, as you hung like a crab, them laughing and her shallow eyes gone.

You pause, pressing the end of the pen sharply against your lower lip, staring across the snowy parking lot. The faculty exit door swings open, and double-em appears there, hunched in his fleece-lined field jacket as he walks to his bike, stoops to unlock it, his breath pluming white in the freezing air.

Reaching across the dashboard, you slip the notebook and pen into the glove compartment, turn the key in the ignition, watching the bike rattle across the lot, out onto the icy road.

You release the emergency brake, clutch, rolling slowly from the parking space, and you think of Harpocrates, god of silence, the silence that leads to triumph. You need only hold your tongue. And dare.

# Chapter Seven

Someone has left a copy of *The Economist* in the little bin on the door of his office and he chucks it into his attaché case to read on the train, lets himself out the faculty door and stoops to unlock his bike. He swings up onto it, rattles across the parking lot and out onto the icy road, bikes up to the Long Island Railroad Station and stands on the freezing platform to wait. For many years, he hated the cold, but as he gets older he begins to appreciate its bitter charm. Dark and cold, immerse yourself in it for short bouts and you feel so alive when you come in out of it.

The train is almost empty. He takes a window seat and watches the station slide away, thinking about Geoff Burns, about his wanting children so much. On the one hand, he understands it. His own life would have been so much poorer without Jimbo and Larry to love, without this aspect of his love for Jenny, their shared experience of creating new lives. Still. He and Jen had been so much younger when they had the kids, in their thirties but still a lot younger than Geoff. They just had them. They wanted them, were glad to have them, but it hadn't been a matter of actual choice. How different it would be to *choose* to have children. To choose a child who was not your own. Pick a child, any child. The entire prospect frightened him because he had doubts and fears, and he did not know how to express them to his friend or whether he should since Geoff had given no opening for it that *he* could discern, and he certainly did not want to do anything to upset their truce.

Outside the window grey trees flash past in a grey white landscape double reflected in the pane with his own face suspended vaguely amidst them. The car door slides open. Twomey glances up and sees cherub-faced young Serafino there. *Please don't sit down.* Serafino merely nods, smiling, and proceeds to the next car, an unlit cigarette between his fingers. *Thank you, Serafino. Extra points for that.*

Twomey snaps open his attaché case, takes out *The Economist.* The spine is bent so it falls open to *The American Survey* section—a series of articles on contemporary crime. Cozy. Twomey pops a peppermint Life-saver into his mouth and starts to read the first sentence of the introduction. "A spate of brutal murders of young children..." He skips to the next which is about the trial of Lorena Bobbit for having cut off the penis of her husband, John Wayne Bobbit. It occurs to Twomey that this is the second murder and maiming case recently involving someone whose forenames are John Wayne. Bobbit and Gacy. Nice legacy for the Duke. The article tells about the circus atmosphere outside the court where tee shirts and chocolate genitalia are being hawked. *Clockwork Orange.* The next article is about the Golly killing Burns just mentioned to him. Someone has written something, underlined something in one of the columns; where the Morrison song "The End" is quoted, these words are highlighted with what looks like mercurochrome: "'Father?' 'Yes, son?' 'I want to kill you.'" and penned in the margin alongside are the words, *Can you dig it, daddy?*

Twomey blinks, looks out the window sees his face in the trees, goes to the next article, sees it is about the Menendez Brothers, thinks, *Fuck this anyway,* and pitches the magazine back into his attaché case.

When the train slides into the station at Woodside, Twomey stares out the frosted window at the familar platform and does not rise. There is an interminable moment where his stomach registers the fact that it is his station yet he is not getting up, still can try, still can try, still... The doors bump shut. *Too late.* The train proceeds toward the East River. *Is this me?* He thinks about sitting in this metal tube and sliding through a tunnel beneath the river. Mystical direction. Moving west. *The west is the best, baby. Get here and we'll do the rest.* Morrison was less a poet than a cabaret artist. Good one. Some great lines. *Why are you doing this? Jenny will have your arse. You have to go back and see your mother.*

At Grand Central he thinks how he would take the IRT back into Queens, towards Flushing, but finds himself climbing the stairs to Eighth Avenue, out past the black guys who stand around watching, hooded, breaths panting from their shadowed faces. He walks north on the freezing avenue, realizes he is looking for a bar, pictures himself in some shabby Irish saloon, tries to figure out where he wants to go. Chumley's? The White Horse? Pete's Tavern? But his feet seem to know precisely where they want to go, and then he is thinking about his father, how he used to love to stop in the Oak Bar for a cocktail. He recognizes the excuse as flimsy but decides to go for it anyway, in Dad's honor.

Late afternoon by the time he places his half-frozen butt onto a stool recognizing that what it takes on such a day, to refresh a tired heart, is an Oak Bar martini in a cocktail glass. Gin, rocks, dash of Noilly Pratt, three olives on a tiny wooden spear, and a little glass dish of quality peanuts. He watches the bartender do his work while he tenderly massages life back into the tip of his frozen nose.

Then the little chalice stands on the bar before him. He raises it to his lips. The uplift is instantaneous. Dry chill across the lips and straight to the brain.

Let this moment last forever, a magic circle within the best bar of the best hotel in the world, surrounded by the gathering darkness of unimpeachable December. Sleigh bells tinkle on the muzak and smarmy voices sing, *Let it snow let it snow let it snow...*

Twomey agrees. Good blizzard do this city good. Whiten the desolate wind belching through the canyons, make his kids happy, make *him* happy. A woman at the next table, wearing a sprig of holly and two red plastic bells pinned to her blouse, has a crooked grin plastered across her mouth. Twomey glances away, sips his gin. He avoids handling the glass, not to melt the ice too quickly, helps himself to peanuts, feels good among all the well-dressed Christmas shoppers with their coats piled behind on their chairs, red-nosed, nests of colorful shopping bags around their feet, living Christmas trees sucking up sweet cocktails. Pot was never as good as this. And acid, well, acid was less subtle than gin.

Yet no matter how he looks into his liquor, straight down or from the side, held up to the light, he sees right through it to what he has promised Jenny he will do today. Still he lingers, studies the level of the drink, considers ordering another, sees Jenny's face in his mind's eye saying, *Another one, Fred?* thinks about Jenny, his boys, the promise to visit his mother, but with sad conviction he recognizes that the promise will require two martinis to fulfill and that that is why he stayed on the train at Woodside. His butt knew enough not to let him stand up; his feet knew where to take him.

*Fred, you let that woman be all alone on Thanksgiving!*

*I know, hon. Shoot me. I deserve it.*

The waiter moves within his field of vision; Twomey raises one finger and both eyebrows, points at his drink, feels in his pocket for bills, thinks once again that he will have to give in and get a cell phone one of these days.

The phone booth is glass and looks one way into the bar, the other out to Central Park South in the dingy snow-less afternoon, winter trees, stone wall, grey boulders, crosstown traffic. Twomey punches in the number he knows as well as his own social security number.

As he listens to the ring, he watches a chestnut-brown horse, nostrils steaming, step past in the road with a policeman on its back, thinks of the time he demonstrated—where the hell was it?—when mounted cops came in to disperse them, all those years ago. His mother's voice, small, suspicious, non-committal, New York-accented, speaks into his ear: "Hello?"

"Mom. It's Freddy."

"Freddy? Are you calling from China?"

"China! We were in Ohio! Canton, Ohio! Mom, we've been back for a year. I spoke to you last month."

"From China!"

"From Farmingville, Mom."

She chuckles. "Excuse me for laughing, Freddy, but I can't imagine you of all people living on a farm. Imagine that."

"It's the suburbs. I drove you out there last summer, don't you remember? We had a barbecue? Try to remember it, Mom."

"I have such a headache."

"Take an aspirin, Mom. Tylenol. Have you been to the doctor's?"

As he speaks this sentence, he lifts his glass to his lips, and someone entering the bar catches his eye. A tall woman in an elegant linen suit the color of champagne, short hair framing her face in an array of delicate black curls. Twomey catches his breath, whispers, "Jesus, Mary, and Joseph," while his mother repeats Dr. Scrivane's detailed analysis of her headache.

"Isn't Scrivane getting kind of old to practise, Mom?"

"Well, he's younger than me, Freddy!"

The woman's gaze sweeps toward the phone booth, and Twomey feels his cheeks redden. He doubts she could have seen him, but she nods, once, curtly, and Twomey lowers his gaze, instantly regretting having done so. Beside her is a man he knows by sight, blue cashmere topcoat over a silver suit, a Dean from the Lincoln Center Campus, a chunky dark man who looks something like a middle-aged Richard M. Nixon. Twomey notes the way the man squeezes her narrow waist as he guides her to a table. Twomey wishes he were home with Jenny and the boys, away from here, away from this phone call and this vision. He thinks, calculates how long it's been since he last saw her, since they broke it off and she moved on from the Long Island campus to bigger and better things in the Big Apple. She looks older, but not very much so. Her skin is still good. The curls on her brow. Eyes large and green. The way her face looks, smiling at her Dean there, envy turns inside him. *Catherine*, he thinks as he tells his mother he will be over shortly, places the phone back in its cradle, experiences an extreme moment of regret that he ever met her, that he saw her again here, that he is forced to remember what knowing her made of him: *You should hear what they say/About you: cheat cheat...*

A picture comes into his mind of his father kneeling to pray in the shadows beside his bed at night. He looks at the band of gold on his finger reflecting light through his gin on the shelf of the phone booth as he lifts the martini to his mouth and watches Catherine in her linen suit watch the Dean who is not her husband. How effortlessly she lied, simply did as she pleased, and kept it to herself. Twomey asked her once if her husband knew. "Of course not," she said. "That would be cruel." Female version of Geoff Burns.

Her boldness seemed a new way of life to him. For a time. For the weeks he carried on with her. Then one evening, over drinks at the Pointview Inn, she told him something, and it occurred to him he had no way of knowing whether she was lying to him. It was an inconsequential matter, something about a cancelled appointment, a change of plans, but he looked into her face and asked, "Are you lying to me, Catherine?"

Her green eyes met his, startled. "Of course not," she said, and he realized he would never, ever know whether she was lying. About anything.

He hates the thought of the rest of his day, the visit to his mother, the Long Island Railroad home to Jenny with the memory of Catherine's face in the Oak Bar, green eyes looking up at the Dean as they once looked at him, the kind of look that could make you feel big—for a while. He dreads that this thing is inside him, a smudge on his life. The only time he had ever really been unfaithful to Jenny. How he wishes he could tell her, be forgiven, be cleansed of it, the way he used to be able to do in confession. Bless me, father, for I have sinned...

He considers that for a moment, considers whether he could go back to it, bring it all out, tell everything. He thinks about the things he would tell, those years especially, those sick years. Nearly ten years of his life that were a mess of error, guilt. From wrong to wrong. But the one main thing, the last thing, when he got out of it. Katey sleeping in the back room, desert sunlight slanting down onto her swollen face.

How old would he be now? Or she? Maybe aborted. Stillborn. And Katey? Dead now? Maybe a good life after all. Good husband. Everyone can get lucky. Make your luck. Maybe well off now, a western matron. Or not well off. Waitress to make ends meet. *What'll it be, honey?* Little green order pad. All the beauty once in her heart. Madness, too. Having to support the kid maybe straightened her out. Kid could support her by now maybe. Be how old? Subtract seventy-one from ninety-three, be twenty-three, twenty-four. If at all. Probably never born. Maybe. And Katey?

He realizes that he is staring through the glass booth at Catherine, and she turns her eyes in his direction, a gaze that is not without

98

warmth, and he sees in it an insult to his wife to whom he owes his loyalty. *Love let us be true to one another...*

It was only a few weeks, a little bit of pleasure. He remembers Burns saying there is no such thing as cheating, you only live once, thing is not to cheat yourself of the few small pleasures available. He thinks of Janet again. The golden fleece of her belly. How close he came. Just last week. *What was I thinking? What the fuck is wrong with me? But I stopped. Didn't go through with it.*

He knows there is no pleasure outside his home anymore. And still there was that smudge. A smudge that tainted this life, the new life he vowed would be so right, wife, children, shoulder to the wheel. The basic truths: You have to get up when the alarm clock rings. You have to get up early and work hard or the others will look at you and say he doesn't get up early and work hard. You have to be faithful to your wife or otherwise there is no faith nor hope nor peace nor certitude nor help for pain...

The waiter brings another round of drinks to Catherine and her Nixon dean. She is smiling, bright as a candle, and her eyes flick in Twomey's direction again, and it occurs to him she would even cheat on her dean, she would cheat on anybody and everybody in a world where there was no faith.

*Come to the window, love, let us be true to one another...*

The IRT Flushing Line screeches around the elevated track, curving up above Bridge Plaza. Face close to the glass of the door window, Twomey watches the Plaza turn past beneath him, sees the polished brass doors of the Metropolitan Insurance Co which as a child he had thought were gold and behind which his father passed the bulk of his adult life. Further on, the Star Hotel, at the door of which a man and woman now stand in the eternal posture: negotiating. A perfect Hopper. The landscape of factories, neon Silvercup letters in the gathering darkness of late afternoon in this place where as a child he rode his bike, rollerskated, fished for killies in the now filled swamp, shoplifted at Sears & Roebuck's, adored his mother, loved his father, his brother. A happy childhood. You had to learn discontent in life, as his brother James had, leaving them as he did, abandoning them to a life that was no longer ideal, a life he invalidated and then left them as a legacy.

His mother peers from behind a police chain as Twomey waits, sucking a mint, thinks about time, which seems suspended like Zeno's arrow, the little units of seconds it takes, half-life of seconds, for the chain to rattle out of its slot, the door to open, his mother's face to appear, body to enter his embrace, affording him time to recover from the shock.

So small and fragile against his palms, within his arms, she seems even smaller, her face older since last he saw her just a couple of months before. His nails bite into his palm with remorse at his own negligence, having put this off. *I couldn't help it.* Her hair is totally white and wild. Twomey himself has just entered what he likes to think of, not with total irony, as what a professor of his used to call late youth. At eighty, she is almost twice his age, a little old woman with a haunted look in her eye which used to twinkle.

The familiar smell of the apartment, neither sweet nor sour, a warm smell, close, closes around him as he shuts the door, watches his mother's fragile vein-corded hands carefully relatch the chain. *You used to be so beautiful, Mom.*

"Would you like a coke, Freddy?" she asks.

He looks at her, looks away, looks again, trying to re-accustom himself to his mother as an old woman. It occurs to him that he does not remember her this way when he is not with her. In his memory, she is still young, still looks a little like Donna Reed.

"You sit down, Mom. Let me make you some tea."

"I'd rather have a Dr. Brown's Cel-Ray tonic."

Twomey in the kitchen pops open the refrigerator door, swears it is the same GE of his childhood, knows it couldn't be, rummages through the bottles and jars there, checks the date on a Hellman's mayonnaise, does a double take. Best if consumed three years ago. As he prises ice cubes from a metal tray, his eye wanders over the array of plastic coasters, scraps of flowered paper, a flank of empty screw top jars, a lopsided, played-out stub of Brillo pad, which fills him with unaccountable sorrow. All at once he knows in his body that he cannot stay much longer.

100

He wanders the living room, a Twomey museum, museum of his childhood, ice cubes clinking in his glass of ginger ale, looking at bookcases, books, knickknacks. A white plaster Our Lady of the Television stands atop the old RCA console, a statuette Twomey won for collecting the most money in the class Might Box Drive of 1957.

Other mementoes are ranked behind the glass of his father's father's bookcases. One of them is filled exclusively with red books. "Who did this, Mom?"

"I'm not sure," she says and sips her Cel-Ray tonic. "I think I did. Do you like it?"

"Nice." He opens a cabinet door and lifts out a little metal Roman chariot he assembled and painted nearly forty years before. He glances at his mother, a little old woman with wild white hair and frightened blue eyes.

"Mom, do you get some help here? Is anyone helping you?"

"Your Uncle Martin comes by frequently."

"What does he do for you?"

She stares at him for a moment. "I can't remember. Isn't that silly?"

The whip wielded by the charioteer is a length of string Twomey soaked in Lepage's glue forty years ago so it would stand up, as if in the arc of a swing behind the Roman's back. And still it stands in arc. Testimonial for Lepage. Twomey holds it close to his face, studies the leather flaps of the charioteer's armor, the ornate handwork on the chariot itself, the wheel hubs. There are other figures Twomey painted, outfitted with armor he had made from bits of cardboard and tin, little cannons, tiny scenes of rebels defending a stone wall Twomey built of pebbles, glue, and grass clumps, cotton smoke pluming from cannons.

He remembers sitting in his room in the old corner house where they lived for his first nineteen years, remembers spreading newspaper across his desk, working with tiny bottles of Pla and number one brushes tweezed to a hair, copying coats of arms from a heraldry catalogue, remembers the smell of glue and paint and thinner, wonders what kind of a kid he was after all, what kind of kid would sit and squint over this junk.

"It's amazing you still save these things, Mom."

"What things?"

"These tin soldiers."

"James was so fond of them."

Twomey sips his ginger ale. "James?"

His mother's eyes lighten in the dust of her face. "Yes, he was so diligent. I'll never forget how he labored with the tiniest details, even their eyes! Why he even painted the eyes! The whites and the irises!"

Twomey sets his glass down on top of a bookcase, beside a jade buddha, picks it up again and wipes away the water ring with his handkerchief, sets the glass down again. He touches the wall for balance as a single word, syllable, simmers in his consciousness: *Me! I made these!* He shuts his eyes tight, sees James in the chair in his apartment, smells him, sees the shattered forehead. No note, no reason, he never even said goodbye, Mom, the poor guy, poor Mom, think if Jimbo or Larry ever, but they wouldn't, never.

Twomey picks up his ginger ale again, sips. "Jenny and the boys send their love, Mom."

He knows the smile she shows him, her polite smile, the smile she used to flash to hold off neighbors she was not in the mood to talk to. "When did you eat last, Mom?"

"Eat?" She is staring at her hand, a tiny fragile thing, turning it over in front of her eyes as if trying to figure out what it's for.

Twomey makes her a cream cheese and olive sandwich on whole wheat bread, puts the tea kettle on and sits staring at a picture of the pieta on the wall, while she eats the sandwich. In a cardboard frame on the sideboard is an oval portrait of his mother's sister, Constance. Twomey remembers her as a cynical woman whose favorite expression when called upon to care about something was, *What is that to me? What is he to me? What are you to me?* Twomey looks at his mother intently munching her cream cheese sandwich, and a thought, a question enters his mind. *What are we to each other? What are any of us to one another? What is the meaning of our life together?* For an instant, the question seems an entry to the core of a great mystery;

then it eludes him, the words go flat, he cannot retrieve the force of their first appearance. It occurs to him that love, emotion is not a thought but a feeling, and that, too, seems a brilliant observation for a moment until he recognizes how obvious it is, and it all slides through his fingers.

From the kitchen, the kettle shrieks. His mother sits at the table making sounds which Twomey slowly recognizes as a song.

She sings, "Seventy-six trombones led the big parade!" She smiles at him. "James phoned me from China on my seventy-sixth birthday to sing that to me."

Twomey pours steaming water over a Lipton flow-through. Should you humor them or not? "Actually it was me, Mom. I phoned. From Canton, *Ohio*. I was visiting professor there and couldn't get home, so I phoned. James was already gone when you turned seventy-six, Mom."

"I wouldn't know about that," she says, warming her hands around the tea mug. Twomey has begun to notice how very quiet it is in the apartment, quiet and still, close. His breathing steepens. He watches his mother's blue hands lift the tea mug to her old woman's mouth.

"How about another sandwich, Mom?"

"Yes!" she says, her face alight. "I want one of those Greek ones!"

"Greek?"

"Yes! Where you take a piece of bread and some cheese and olives and *then*: another piece of bread."

"Is that Greek?" he asks, spreading cheese on whole wheat.

She stares at him. "Well, why?"

Twomey just smiles. "It's okay, Mom," puts the sandwich in front of her, pours more tea.

"I'm so hungry," she says. "I haven't eaten all day." She reaches into her mouth, removes a piece of metal bridgework and puts it on the table, nudges it with her fingertip as though it might begin to crawl, mutters, "Damnation." Twomey watches her eat, watches her begin to collect crumbs from the plate on her fingertip.

"Mom, Jenny and the kids and I are looking forward to your coming for Christmas this year. I'll drive you out. Jenny ordered a

103

great big bird."

She blushes. "Well, that's awfully sweet of you, Freddy, but I already promised James. I always have Christmas with James. He would be disappointed." She lowers her voice. "Otherwise he'd be all alone, you know."

Twomey smiles, thinking. "Well, James could come, too. It'd be great!"

She shakes her head slowly, skeptically. "I just don't know, Freddy. I'll have to discuss it with him before I say one way or the other."

Beneath the edge of the table, Twomey looks at his watch, says, "I'll have to be off now, Mom."

She pecks up a crumb and deposits it in her palm. "Be sure to give my love to James," she says, "and don't forget the Bufferin. I have such a headache!"

"Mom, I've got to go. Do you want me to call Uncle Martin?"

"He's such a prick," she mutters. "He said mean things to me and hit me, but my father gave him a good talking to."

"Uncle Martin loves you, Mom."

"Perhaps," she says and tips her head back with a blithe expression on her face. "Perhaps. With linen napkins on their laps. They loved me with a hundred hates, the dinner heaped upon their plates..."

"It's fantastic how you can remember poems, Mom. Do you still hear from any of your old students, that girl, woman, what was her name, that always brought you flowers at Easter?" She does not answer, seems not to have heard. He is in the foyer, pulling on his coat as he asks this and hears her begin to sing again, low in her throat, a tuneless, gravelly murmur which he finally recognizes as "The September Song."

"Dad used to love that," he says.

She stares at him. "He did? No, I don't think so. He liked 'Miss Fogarty's Christmas Cake' and that other one, that terrible, vulgar one about the goose."

Twomey chuckles, sings, "Don't give me no goose for Christmas, Grandma/Stop it/Cut it out/Now don't you dare..."

"Stop that!" she hisses at him, furious. Startled, he crouches by the armchair where she sits, puts his arms around her. "Hey, Mom, it's okay, don't worry, Mom." She sits stiffly in his embrace, like a child humoring an affectionate parent. It occurs to him that he can not remember the last time she so much as mentioned his father. Her husband. He remembers the wake, the funeral more than twenty-five years before. In the beginning, she used to talk about him: Your father this, your father that. He thinks back on their life, what he saw of it, tries to remember affectionate moments between them. He wonders if she still misses him, still feels love for him, would like to ask, but fears upsetting her, knows he cannot stay to try to calm her again if she gets upset.

He climbs slowly down the stairs and into the street, the papery feel of his mother's forehead on his lips, the lines of her poem ringing through his brain.

The light is gone. A few scattered flakes of snow float on the cold dark air above his bare head. He stops at the corner, knots his scarf around his throat, spots a flat empty wine bottle in the gut-ter. He stoops for it, studies the dirty, cold glass against his palm, the dirt-smeared Thunderbird label, pictures some bum, some lost abandoned man, huddled in a freezing doorway, sucking from this bottle. Abruptly, he smashes it against the dark brick wall beside the Chinese laundry, shielding his face from the spray of glass.

He ducks out onto the avenue, beneath the El, grateful for the rumbling IRT that fills his brain, his body, plugs his ears from thought.

Snow falls lightly as he steps out of the train onto the Farmingville platform. You can see the dark platform through the thin coating of snow, and he steps carefully down to the street, around to where his bike is locked, the seat and handlebars and fenders dusted white. He stoops to turn the dial of the lock, notices the rear wheel is flat, the front wheel, too. He hunkers there in the cold, not yet angry for the sight has frightened him too much, the thought that someone might be out to get him. Who? Nonsense. Utter nonsense. With the realization that it is utter nonsense, his anger breaks, and he kicks the chain link fence to which the bike is chained, mutters a string of curses, reaches for the pump but it is not there. He hesitates, tries to remember whether he clipped it back to the cross bar after pumping Jimbo's bike this morning, stoops again, unlocks the bike.

There is a bike shop down the street from the station. He leaves the bike there and phones for a taxi from the booth by the station, waits in there watching the snow fall along the street, layering trees and fences, window ledges, parked cars, parking meters. He sees a young man on a bike turn the corner, hunched against the falling snow; the bike wobbles in a snow rut, disappears down the avenue. Was that Jimbo?

The chill seeps up his pant legs, in under the cuffs of his coat. His forehead aches. He thinks about getting a hat. Maybe a cap. One of those Irish ones.

A black and white taxi rolls in alongside the curb, and Twomey hurries into the warm interior, shivering.

As he pulls up outside his house, he sees Jenny in the alley talking to Leo Zilka. They stand alongside his red T-bird. Zilka is wearing a red lumberjack and Jenny is in a house dress, hugging her arms for warmth. She touches Zilka's arm and steps over the clumpy snow back to their own alley just as Twomey pays and gets out of the taxi.

"Hi, hon? What's up with Leo?"

She shakes her head. "I'm freezin'!" In the warm house, she says, "I think he's not quite over the divorce yet."

"So the T-bird didn't soothe his hurt? He still needs comfort?"

"Did you see your mother?" Jenny asks.

"Yes, sure."

"How is she?"

He shrugs, measuring gin, vermouth, spearing olives. "You want?" She nods. "Mom is not a young woman, Jen."

As the gin steams over the crackling ice, he recalls the face of Catherine gazing up at her dean and feels dirt in his heart, and wishes to God he could tell her, beg forgiveness, but knows it is too dangerous to open that can of worms, and he knows he will not do it, thinks idly about all the big jets at JFK and how it would be to stick his head into one of the turbos as it revs up. He thinks about telling her his bike was flat again, decides not to, wonders what that means. "Is Jimbo home?" he asks.

Taking the drink from him, she nods. "In his room."

"When did he get in?"

"I'm not sure. I was out most of the afternoon. Fitness center. Why?"

He shakes his head, raises his glass.

"Did you invite her for Christmas dinner?" Jenny asks.

He nods. They are sitting in leather frame chairs by the front window. He sees lights in the windows of the other houses along the street, feels some comfort in the expanse of his lawn, thinks about how much it would cost to put his mother in a home, wonders if the money they would get selling her co-op would cover it, considers the alternative. Jenny once indicated she would, but that was some time ago, and anyway, he can't, he can't have her live here, and the certainty of the knowledge makes him wonder who he is now, finally, at the age of forty-eight. He wonders what it is about Jenny that she might be willing to do it, to try at least, while he would not. Would she just force herself? What was the difference between them?

"Well?" Jenny asks impatiently.

Twomey raises his glass in salute. They sip. "She said she already promised James." Jenny stares at him. "She always has Christmas with James, you see. But she'll talk to him and let us know."

"You have to explain to her, Freddy."

He nods, whispers, "I told her James could come, too," looks surreptitiously at her, sitting about five feet away from him in her chair, calculating what moves it would take for him to bridge that distance, thinking about the slight, feisty little girl she was how many years ago when they met on the beach at Hampton Bays, and he sang to her so she smiled, *Jenny Jenny Jenny won't you come along with me...* He puts his drink down on the drum table, sits forward. Their eyes meet.

He can see her register his intention, as she says, "Help!", dodges up from her chair into the kitchen. He sighs, wonders if this is the beginning of the end for them.

But in bed that night she responds to his touch. Jim Morrison on the radio sings, *Hello, I love you, won't you tell me your name?* and Twomey looks down into Jenny's grey eyes, whispers, *Jenny Jenny*

*Jenny*. Her mouth opens in pleasure, snowlight on her teeth, and he says, "I love you, Jenny."

She doesn't answer. Not that he thinks her silence is intentional, but even so, it saddens him, and he feels as though her body's response, too, is faint, faked even, but no, he knows what is really happening here, he knows that the layer between them can only be his own guilt, the image of Catherine, that smudge...

Afterwards she falls asleep on her side, her back to him. He switches off the radio, lies watching the dark ceiling, remembers Catherine's eyes in the Oak Bar, thinks of his mother, his father, wonders again if she still misses him sometimes, if she thinks tenderly of him. He wonders if she was ever glad to be free of him, and what that means, whether it matters. The gauze curtains float in a draft of chill night air. He tucks the covers up around Jenny's shoulder, leans over to study her face, the wide pretty mouth, the almond, almost Asian shape of her eyes. A novel question enters his thoughts: he wonders if she ever cheated on him, tries to remember times where there might have been opportunities, men with whom she might have wanted to. The thought of her in another man's bed, another man's hands on her, brings a tightness to his chest. Behind his curtained eyes, he sees a big shadowed body on top of her, a man's face between her legs, her palms holding the back of his head there, her hand holding his prick, her open mouth moving down... Water stings his eyes. He knows he deserves no better, wonders if, really, in the scheme of things, it would matter. He remembers again Burns saying that what matters is not to cheat yourself of life. So glib. So easy. He pictures Burns making moves on Jenny. Pictures his hand sliding into her blouse, remembers them dancing once at a faculty party, Geoff's paw low on her back, partly on her butt really, and Jenny let it be there... No. He will not entertain such thoughts. Jenny never would. She wouldn't even look at him, the lousy cheat. And what are you, yourself, Twomey, but a cheat? Does it matter? What might really matter, he thinks, would be not the act so much as the lie, the secret life intruding between them. And the thought of a secret life opens other doors again. He thinks of Catherine in the Oak Bar and Janet in Vermont and then all the way back to the desert, those wild years with Katey, then leaving her there like that, trying to get away, took years to find a way, back to the life that would have been his if the sixties hadn't happened to him.

Downstairs, he makes the last drink of the night, trying to calculate which number it is as the gin cracks the cubes. It is long enough since he was last drunk that he is not worried. He wanders barefoot through the dark house, not discontent. He has nothing to be discontent about really; only he wishes he could have just stayed a little longer with his mother, wishes he could somehow have done something for her. What good would it have done to stay another hour? He thinks with fear about if he would ever have to clean her if she soiled the bed, thinks about his Uncle Martin. He had always found Martin somewhat irritating, a fussy thick-lipped man who often nagged Twomey about his hair and his clothes and his stud-ies those first months after Twomey's father died and he was still in college. He tries now to compare himself to Martin, and it occurs to him he no longer knows quite who he is. Did I ever know? Do I have choices? Can I help being whoever the hell it is I am, the kid who painted toy soldiers, whose mother is so old now, who had all those screwed up years before getting any kind of reasonable life started, whose kids are growing up, who cheated on his wife and has to carry that around?

At the big front window he stares across the lawn, registers the fact that it is still snowing. Big flakes fall steadily down the dark sky, and he smiles, remembering how the boys used to cheer when they woke in the morning to find the world covered in snow. He thinks again about Jimbo, about the touchiness between them. Got to try to calm myself down, not let it get to me. He remembers Jimbo as a boy again, how sweet he was. Larry always a little wilder, but a good kid, straight-shooter. They're good boys, both of them. Better than I deserve.

They are growing away from him, both of them, he knows, espe-cially Jimbo. He thinks of his mother in her apartment thinking of her dead son, Twomey's dead brother who shot himself in the head for reasons only he knew.

He wants to go up to speak to Jimbo with whom he had been

so close for so many years. He had been warned this kind of thing would happen by more experienced fathers he knew, though he had doubted it, believed the love between him and *his* kids was stronger than nature.

He makes it to the top of the stairs, but stops outside Jimbo's door, realizes he can't allow himself to tap on the door, wake the boy up to see his father standing there all ginned up and sentimental. He traces his steps back down the stairs, sits watching the snow fall outside. He reaches for the tv remote, switches it on, zaps until he finds something. Discovery channel. Something about elephants on an African plain. A baby elephant, new-born, that can't quite stand. Its feet are misshapen so it walks with the front feet bent backward. Like walking on the front of your wrists or front of your ankles. The herd is moving on, toward water, but the mother and her nine-year-old daughter come back for the new-born, shade it from the sun while it tries to get up. They reach down with their trunks to try to help it stand and it comes up for a moment but then the feet bend back again and it limps along like that toward the water hole. Twomey finds it uncomfortable to watch, zaps the screen into blankness again.

His drink is nearly empty, and he considers mixing another, stares out at the snow, falling perfect as a picture, fat white flakes against a navy blue night, falling falling falling falling. He nods off, wakes again, and in the moment of waking, he remembers that Jimbo has a camoflauge hat, wonders blearily why he thinks of that just now, as his eyelids droop and his head tips forward again and he floats off into a dream, wakes again and realizes he doesn't need another drink.

He hoists his aging body up and shuffles to the hall, to the door behind which Jenny Jenny Jenny sleeps, the snow of a blizzard clicking against the windows, as he remembers again how it was with the boys at the big front window, seeing the lawn white with virgin snow, cheering.

## Shadow King

The Chevy rides the spiraling curves down into the parking cellar beneath the mall. Surrounded by dirty bare concrete walls, you sense a familiar desolation moving inside you, like a memory of dread so close that it has become a friend, cherished even as your hatred of the walls of the last system you were in. Far away now. Those days before you found the way to the True Will.

The ramp gives out to a concrete floor and you nose the Chevy into a space between two pillars. Cut the ignition and sit in the silence, hands on the wheel, thinking, Never get your ass in stir. Keep out. You got to do this thing, reverse the wave, and where it leads you go, but you walk the line, no stir, never, no shut rooms.

You stare over the wheel at the concrete wall and can see the walls of Stockton Home, your last place. They called it a space, not a room, not a cell, a space, and they never bothered to paint over the walls that were covered with the words of boys before you:

*Mother fuck day*
*mother fuck night*
*mother fuck death*
*mother fuck life*

And:

*FUCKED UP FUCKED OVER FUCKED.*

And:

*I got the feva in my fingas*

Even now as you stare at these walls, it is as though you are within them again, the nights, fighting the edge of terror at being locked in this cube. A box. Walls, a door, locked shut, a slot, also shut, no window, ceiling low over your face, the dream of it sliding down, pressing against your mouth as you try to breathe.

Then the buzzer, and the light goes out so the box sits in the dark where you lie, shapes emerge when you study it, movements in your eyes, that you try to describe but can only just almost see always out the side of your eye or even if you shut them it's the same, with your eyes shut or open it's the same.

You never knew if the others would come. How they could get in, the custodian with the flat nose let them, for a price, and he listened, everyone knew he stood outside and listened and fucked his own greasy hand. Sometimes you were asleep and then you woke, and it was the same dark but now you knew someone was there, three, four of them in the dark and you opened your mouth to scream but it was covered so all you heard was your own muffled groaning and their breath, their muttered words.

Sometimes people came from the Red Cross library. It all seemed like an accident when you think about it. Red Cross, like you were some kind of foreigner in some disaster camp and, yeah, how else to describe it? These two people were like gods, you did nothing to turn them from you, a short-haired woman with a flat round face and sack of a body, a skinny guy with a hook in his spine and pimples. They had power over you, and they liked that with their soft voices, concerned eyes, what they wanted was the power, even if maybe they didn't really know that, and you went with it because they had something. They had books.

It could only have been a mistake 'cause these books were like not prime. Some old beat up crummy novels, little bit on religion, positive thinking kind of shit, the almanac was good, but that was always on loan. You got one book a week, and you took what you could get because other than the school books that's all you got. But this one time, somehow, it was an accident, must have been or else, figure it, an arrangement of the Secret Master, why not? The Red Cross, the Rose Cross. The Rosy Crucifixion.

However, it happened, you got this one called *BOOK FOUR* someone didn't screen out, and the white tape label pasted on the spine said *philosophy*, but you could feel some power curling out of it into your palms and in the first lines you glanced at: "Every man is a condemned criminal, only he does not know the date of his execution."

You stole the book. It was easy. They were easy, the flat-faced woman and hooked-back guy, like a round-ball fake out; they were slow.

That was when things started to change. That was when you could begin to transfer space and light into doorways that led down inside yourself. The dark box in which you spent your nights fitted into the hand of a Secret Master who was your Holy Guardian Angel, and then he had True Will and Magick, and everything was different.

You smack shut the car door, cross to the elevator. A man and woman step in beside you, holding hands, their faces flushed from the cold and shining with happiness. As the elevator jolts into motion and lifts slowly, you close your eyes and slip your fingers inside your shirt to touch the copper chain next to your skin. Copper for love of the true intention, chain to bind the wandering mind to True Will.

Open your eyes again when the elevator doors bump open, and watch the young couple join the streaming crowd in the mall. Consider the emotion they rouse in your heart, consider the trap emotion is until you discipline it to your service. To yearn for the end of loneliness is only more illusion for we are all, always, alone. That yearning is itself only part of the darkness that would break into the circle of will—a darkness within reflected from without.

Breathe slowly, deeply, feel the calm enter you.

Strolling through the crowded lanes of shoppers, you survey the products offered for sale, mindful of the four things you wish to buy. To your left just ahead is a cosmetics counter tended by a dark-haired dark-eyed woman, wearing a name badge that says Laura. Her face is thick with make-up over pitted skin, but there is an appealing quality to her features, at once haunted and vulnerable. You stop, pick out a tube of pink lipstick, same shade as last time, to reinforce the message, just in case. Watch the woman as she slips the tube into a little bag, works the cash register, your eyes intent on her, practising. Her awareness of your gaze is palpable even as her eyes evade you. Wait as she hands you the bag, takes the bills you extend to her. When she

113

returns your change you touch the side of her hand with the tips of your fingers, lightly but distinctly, and her eyes lift to yours. Make a magical gesture with your fist, pass it across your chest. She blinks, and you feel the electric charge of power in your heart.

"Your eyes are sad, Laura," you say softly and watch the blood color her cheeks.

In a candle shop named Living Lights, you buy nine pewter candle lamps and ask the woman there for eighteen beeswax votive candles. She glances at you.

"Ideally," you say, "the lamps should burn the fat of slain enemies in each of the pentagrams to keep off the forces of darkness that might break in. But I'll have to make do with beeswax."

Her smile is a grimace as she turns, reaches up to the shelf for the candles. Consider the effect. You have not been sufficiently cunning, have touched her too harshly too quickly. Learn.

The final purchase is in a lingerie department. Take your time, enjoy the array of garments designed to be so close to the magical 'k'. *Kteis*. Pick through a rack displaying bra and panties on hangers, white, black, blue, sheer material, net, silk.

Tiny white silk bikinis. Just like the others. The feel of them excites your fingers, such power in them, to excite, to destroy. Like last time, wear them for a day or two, to authenticate them, prepare them for their work in case another application is necessary.

"*Kteis,*" you say to the blond woman at the cash register.

She tilts her head, smiling.

"*Kteis*. Magick." And smile so innocently she has to return the smile even if you let the words hang unexplained in the air between you. Simplicity of power. Power of simplicity.

Laura helps build the altar in your room, made sacred now, made ready for that which has been meant to come for all these years, ever since the book was delivered into your hands. Nine pentagrams, each with a pewter lamp burning a beeswax candle and in the center the Holy Oblation on which you consecrate the intention of your will.

114

She shivers as you paint the signs on her skin with chicken blood. Then, wearing the silk panties to infuse them with the spirit of lust and the antelope helmet on your head, you circle the altar thrice, chanting, before climbing up and mounting her, watching her eyes through the mask as they melt to your will, feeding your power.

# Chapter Eight

There is a festive mood amongst Twomey's students in the AV lab while he squats before the video, spooling to find the spot in the film he is looking for. He has borrowed a video of *Taxi Driver,* they didn't have the DVD, and wants to use a particular scene to illustrate a point about language and reality, but at the moment he wishes he could just listen to the Bernard Herrmann sound track all by himself with a glass of red wine and a baguette.

"Dr. Twomey? Could I ask a question?"

Twomey glances over his shoulder at the beachboy-faced kid. Serafino. Nice-enough kid really. Weird name. Eye-taliano. "Let me just get this set up first, okay?"

He finds the scene he wants, where Harvey Keitel is sweet-talking Jodie Foster to make her forget her desire to get away from him, stops the video there, faces the class. Serafino has an imploring look on his face, like he wants to be excused to take a pee. "Mr. Serafino?"

"Dr. Twomey, do we get extra credit if we attended the NWP convention?"

Twomey takes a deep breath. Are you putting me on? He concentrates on keeping his voice level. "Students have the privilege of participating in the convention with the idea that it might be a good experience for you, for those of you who are thinking of going further with writing in grad school. For those of you who don't know, the NWP is the national association of college writing programs. The convention was held last week. There were speakers on various creative and organizational topics and participants got to brush shoulders with a lot of people, to start building a network." On some level he is asking himself why he bothers making this phony pitch, but on some other level he knows full well why: to keep Serafino at bay. He glances at the boy. "I trust you got a little benefit out of the experience," he says and plunges on before the boy can answer. "Now let's get to business. Let's watch this scene with Harvey Keitel. Mr. Green, would you mind killing the lights there."

Green smirks slightly as he half stands, reaches to jab the switches, and Twomey punches the machine's power button. He puts it on pause. "Remember now, this is the scene just after DeNiro has tried to help her get away from Keitel, from 'Sport,' and from being used as a prostitute." He starts the film again.

Harvey Keitel and Jodie Foster are in an apartment. Jodie Foster is skeptical, distracted, but somehow close to breaking free. Harvey Keitel holds her, kneeling by her feet.

"You're just tense, that's all," he says.

"I don't like what I'm doing, Sport."

"Oh, baby, I never want you to like what you're doing. If you like what you're doing you wouldn't be my woman. You miss your man, don't you? I got to tend to business. I depend on you. I'd be lost without you. Don't you ever forget that. How much I need you."

He is murmuring into her ear now as they dance to a romantic record played on a cheap stereo, "I want every man to know what it's like to be loved by a woman like you." Her skepticism fades, she melts into him.

"Lights!"

There is a collective moan of disappointment.

"You can all stay and see the whole thing afterwards if you want, but first I want to discuss this scene. Mr. Green, would you hit the lights, please." Twomey sits on the edge of the desk, watches Green smirk as he does what he's been asked. Twomey notes the hard lines of the man's face, wonders about him. Ex-con maybe. "Okay," he says, "Who wants to talk about the function of language in the scene we just saw?"

"Clear case of seduction," says Slovak.

"Head jam," JoAnne Iacono throws in.

Someone sings in a smarmy voice, "Ho, no, don't fug wit my hawt."

"Power!" Serafino blurts. Twomey is interested. Serafino does not generally get so involved in a question. He nods approvingly, sees the blue beachboy eyes remember themselves, his face assume a mask of shyness. Twomey finds himself uncertain, realizes he has not thought his way through this sufficiently. Of course, seduction and power are the obvious answers, the basic answers here. "Yes," he says. "Basically. Right. What else? Deeper. More, excuse the expression, intellectual?"

Nothing. It's like some kind of guessing game. If you want them to get it you have to give them a clue. "Look at it another way, who is the author of this film?"

"Paul Schrader," says grinning Gatszy. Film buff.

"Okay, yes, but I was thinking of Scorsese. Let's say Scorsese is the artist of the film. But who then is the artist of the scene we've just watched? The creator?"

"Keitel," says Slovak.

"Creating what?"

"Her will," says JoAnne Iocono.

"Her mind," Serafino says, again with a certainty that encourages Twomey to new expectations. "Her reality," Serafino adds.

Twomey stabs an index finger at the boy. "Bingo!"

In the lounge he sips a cup of coffee, wondering why he drinks coffee, and thinks uncomfortably about the class. He wonders whether he really understood the scene he has just tried to teach. He had to bluff his way through the last part of the class and couldn't help but feel that half the students grasped the scene more clearly than he himself had. Getting over-focused in your thinking, Twomey.

Across the broad room of tables he sees Slovak and JoAnne Iacono walking together with trays, Serafino several steps behind. Twomey watches to see if they sit together, sees Serafino veer off, take a place by himself near the tall screen windows. Green comes from the line carrying a coffee mug and sits by himself near the wall, his hard-lined face hunched over a student newspaper.

Twomey's morning hangs inside him like a failure. He feels gloomy, staring out the big screened window at the sunless afternoon, tries to cheer himself considering the fact that this is his last class of the week. Free till Monday. Not a bad life. It has been some time since he has written anything, but he has papers to grade, several books to read, two to review. One of them for the *Times*. Good money there. The other for *American Book Review*—a paltry fifty bucks, but fair exposure, chance to get said what you want to say. Sometimes opens a door. That lead piece on Auster stirred a reaction that led to some good contacts, gig or two, reading in the Midwest and a permanent reprint in *Contemporary Literary Criticism*. Permanent as long as CLC exists anyway.

His stomach rumbles. He realizes he is hungry, thirsty, decides to buy himself a baguette and a bottle of mountain red to entertain himself and Jenny with this evening.

He rises, looking forward to his bike ride home, remembers his bike is in the shop. He walked to school, half an hour, rather than ask Jenny to give him a lift (why? afraid to stir her paranoia? or some other reason?) Now he has to walk to the shop, another half hour. Do you good. Earn your wine. Some air in the lungs, move a little. Maybe have a bit of cheese with the wine later. Stilton maybe. Good old footy taste. Give dear Jenny a kiss on the rump in bed tonight. No, not a good idea—turn her off that way. Got to find a way to make it more exciting for her. Her love-making has seemed distracted the past couple times. Is she tired of me? Understandable after all these years. But the fact is I'm not tired of her. Far from it. Jenny, honey, stay with me. Let us be true to one another...

# Chapter Nine

As he locks his bike outside the fitness center, sunlight from behind him suddenly brightens, warming his shoulders and bare head. His mood lifts. Then the light and warmth fade again and the surge of well-being drains away.

Through the double glass doors, and he shows his card, gets a locker key from the smiling Nico at the desk who greets him like a long lost brother. "Hello, Professor Twomey! Long time I no see you and Mrs. Jenny!"

"Well you know how it is, Nico. Overworked and underpaid."

"But you should no forget thee physique, professor. Thee health."

"You're right as rain, Nico."

Jogging down the stairs to the locker room Twomey passes a red-haired woman with black eyebrows and thinks about a guy he knows from the department, guy named Milton, who is obsessive about women, feeds his ego on them. "Check out the eyebrows," Milton told him once. "The eyebrows show the true color. Go for the red eyebrows." And he kissed his fingers to his lips, then let them fly away. They were drinking a beer. Twomey said, "Malt does more than women can to justify God's ways with Milton," and his colleague laughed merrily. It occurs to Twomey he has never seen Milton unhappy. He is a clever critic, his books do well, he gets to be chairman of everything he goes into, and he wallows in women. What about Milton's wife? How does she take it? His second wife actually. Maybe she likes it. Encourages him. Makes him tell her about it. Maybe she has her own lovers. Or maybe Milton's lovers lever her levers. Give myself an orgasm anytime. Good one. Put a crooked smile on the

121

little hammered face. Think of Burns and his wife. Thing is not to cheat yourself. Does everyone do it?

Mystery, all of it, he thinks, as he pulls on his shorts, smacks shut the locker, goes out into the exercise room, warding off a fleeting memory of Montpelier with the protection of a mental cross. From up above he hears the many feet of an aerobic session pounding the floor to some kind of electronic hip hop as he hangs backwards on an incline bench doing half sit-ups.

Everything was so fine last night. He got home, put everything out of his mind, refused to think about it, any of it. He finally unpacked his bag from Montpelier, threw his laundry down the cellar stairs. He and Jenny shared a bottle of Beaujolais Villages and made love—even if she still seemed less than enthusiastic, or rather her enthusiasm seemed unnatural, faked—and he woke this morning feeling like a new man. Then, as he sat drinking coffee and reading the paper, she came up from the basement laundry room with a strange light in her eye and asked, "So how was the conference anyway? You only told me about Geoff Burns there, not about what you did." Something odd was in her voice.

He shrugged. "Just...the usual."

"Oh? Do you usually get a blow job?"

She was staring at him. He studied her face. There was no joke on it. Then she pitched something white at him, two things that began to separate in the air, and he caught them by reflex, one-handed, his briefs. Smeared all around the fly was pink lipstick. And something else white. A pair of women's silk panties.

"No," he said. "Uh uh. No way."

"Like a trout in the milk, honey? Don't take me for a fool, okay?" Her tone was surprisingly mild—which somehow frightened him more than if she was furious.

"Jenny, no. Believe me, no. Someone is fucking over me. Look." He went into his room, got his journals out of his bag, opened to the page from Vermont. "I did not write these sentences. Someone got into my room. Someone is playing an ugly game. Someone got into my room and did these things. Listen, the sentences written

122

there were also spray-painted on a mailbox at the conference. And as I think back over it, there were other things too. Punctured tires. Do you remember all the flats on my bike? And something else...that that that time with the steak knife in the doll's hand on your sculpture model? Remember? The the the thing I saw, in the garden."

Jenny watched him. She took the shorts from him, bunched up in one hand. The panties. "And these?"

He shook his head, desperately helpless to explain.

"Just tell me the truth. I can take it. Was there a woman?"

"There was no woman," he said and heard his voice sail across the sentence without a hitch. And then the lie, no, the half-lie was told. It was only a half-lie but he recognized in the moment, the way she took it, believed, that there was a price, there would be a price for this. Even if she never found out, it had already cost him something. And if she found out later, the more time that passed the more the interest would compound. You're in it now, asshole. Tell the truth! Tell! But his lips did not part.

"You know that story about Geoff Burns," Jenny said. "Are you sure you weren't talking about yourself? Be a grown-up, Fred. Be a man, can't you?"

"Be a man? For Christ's sake, Jenny. There *was* no woman." Twice-told lie. No going back now.


He lays back, agreeably depleted after the hundredth sit up, feels the sweat on his forehead, inside his tee shirt. Come on, endorphins, set me free.

He fits two twenty-pound plates on each end of the bench press bar, lies back on the padding. He grips the bar, prepares himself for the weight, thinks, But if it wasn't Janet, then who? He asked her straight out, caught her alone in the TA room and apologized for his behavior.

"It's okay," she said. "I understand. You're married. You have children. Your wife's lucky. A lot of men wouldn't have thought twice."

"I'm lucky," he said.

"You give good kisses."

"Janet..." He didn't want to ask. "I'm really sorry to ask this,

123

but I have to. Did you go in my room at all? Write something in my notebook? Put something on...a piece of my clothing?"

"On...what? What are you talking about?"

And just like that, the cozy friendliness of understanding vanished. Now on some level they were enemies, he could see it. She hated him. Because she had done nothing. He could see that clearly in her face, her response. Yet he had made himself strange in her eyes. Whoever is out to get him is getting him good. In many directions.

He lifts the bar off the brace, feels the tightening of his chest and back, his triceps. He lowers, lifts, lowers, lifts, sucking in air, blowing out. Eight reps, nine... The tenth is slow. He almost can't, but must. Pushes, gets the bar back onto the brace with a jarring rattle of metal, lays there panting, his face soaked.

Who then if not Janet? Surely Burns is not that far out. Or is he? Twomey recalls again the tight anger of the man's smile next morning, the attack. Is he in love with Janet? Or was it just hurt pride? Did he plant some subtle doubt in Jenny's mind? Could a normal man invest so much in losing an opportunity to be with a woman that he would become pathological? No, surely this is unreal. Couldn't be Burns, could it? But if it wasn't Burns and wasn't Janet, then who?

Or was it Janet anyway? That would be a really weird twist there.

His pulse is low and steady as he bikes slowly across the snowy green toward the college. The tightness of his muscles renews his sense of himself, of his capability as a man. The challenge of who is trying to disturb his life seems less menacing, more of a mere puzzle to work with, or to abandon. The latter thought intrigues him. How to abandon it? Ignore it? Move? Perhaps it would just stop. This line of thought, he feels, is leading to some dark place. He turns his mind from it, gazes up at the row of houses he is passing, each with its drear December patch of lawn, faces dull with winter beneath a grey-white sky in which a pale wafer of moon is still visible. The moon brings him back to his task this morning, manuscript conferences with Alan Serafino and then Xavier Green. Serafino's story begins with an image of a man rising to look out the window and see in the sky one sun and two moons. Twomey instantly recognized the power of the image, sidelined the sentences, jotted "good" in the margin. The story goes on to follow the man through his day. The man is trying to find his son whom he has never met. He has reason to believe that his son is nearby, one of the many unknown faces that people his everyday life. He suspects that his son may know who he is, but chooses not to reveal himself to his father. The father has only a few facts to go on: the date and place of birth, a scar of mangled skin beneath the left pectoral ("Heart scars?" Twomey wrote in the margin). The father searches like a detective, goes into a diner, questions the young counterman there, talks to a policeman parked in a patrol car, a tie salesman, two young men at the office where he works. At the end of the day he stops in a restaurant for dinner, drinks a bottle of wine, staggers ("On *one* bottle?") out of the restaurant, goes into an alley to urinate and someone is waiting for him there, the blade of a knife leaps out to glint, reflecting the moon ("Two moons?") The mugger demands everything he has. The man, whose penis is still out, lunges at the mugger. They struggle over the knife, but the older man is heavier, turns the blade toward the mugger's heart, leans his weight to it. The mugger dies smiling weirdly into the man's face. As the body falls still beneath him, the man realizes that he is excited, his penis is erect. He feels both triumphant and ashamed, but also alarmed that he has killed someone. He tears open the young man's shirt to examine the wound, discovers a mangled scar beneath the left pectoral, just beside where the knife blade has slid into the young man's heart. The man goes into the boy's pocket, gets his wallet, finds a card with his place and date of birth: they match. He has killed his own son.

A voice from the end of the alley orders him to freeze. The police. The man is arrested, having been caught sitting over the body of a young man he has stabbed to death, the boy's wallet in his hands, apparently about to commit an act of necrophilia. It ends with the man handcuffed in the back of the police car. One of the policemen looks back at him with disgust. "You sick bastard," he mutters as the man looks out the window up at the sky with its two moons.

Serafino has titled the story "A Passion in the Desert." Twomey looks at the title, inclined to sideline it and write, "Why use Balzac's title here?" wondering indeed whether Serafino is fully aware it is Balzac's title, feels he should consider it further. He thinks about the fact that Serafino saw him in the hall at the conference in Vermont when he came out of Janet's room. He recalls the chill expression on the young man's face and despite himself is embarrassed. Will the boy push it? None of his business. It occurs to him suddenly, with such violence that he almost topples his bike rounding the downhill curve over a patch of frozen leaves towards the building where his office is, that Serafino might be the one who is stalking him. He has not used the word before, "stalking," and it comes to him now with a mixed sense of terror and relief; giving a name to what is being done to him seems to make it somehow more manageable, but at the same time injects it with a sense of menace beyond what he has yet allowed himself to regard it with. A systematic terrorization. To what end? He pictures Serafino's face, shakes his head as he steers the bike across the parking area toward the entrance of the red brick building. No. True, Serafino had been there at the Conference, as had Xavier Green and he saw a couple other of his students as well. But Serafino had been in the hall when he left Janet's room, might have known the door was Twomey's, might have tried it, found it unlocked… There was possible opportunity then. But why? What motive?

If it was someone in his class, Twomey would put his money on Green, ex-con looking guy. But why? As he loops the chainlock through his rear wheel and around the cross bar to a steel signpost, snaps the bolt shut, feeling the chill steel against his momentarily bare fingers, an image of Jimbo's face enters his mind, and it occurs to him he does not know where Jimbo was last weekend. He could ask. Just ask. What'd you do last weekend, son? Anything of interest? The fake telephone number. Fake? Or just hastily scribbled?

This is absurd. What about the other students who were there in Vermont? Green? Couple of girls? This is absurd. Make a list. Question them. Absurd nonsense.

But still.

Something *has* happened. Something *is* going on.

# Chapter Ten

Serafino sits in the low slung visitors chair beside Twomey's desk, smoking a ballpoint pen as Twomey goes into his spiel.

"There is so much to admire here, Alan, so many truly powerful details, and the story itself as such is utterly intriguing. So I want you to take as the background of everything else I am about to say to you that I am full of praise and admiration for what you've accomplished here. Okay?"

Serafino removes the pen from between his lips and taps imaginary ash into an ashtray full of marbles. He imitates Groucho Marx. "I think I'm about to get my ass kicked."

Twomey laughs. "On the contrary. If you can listen to what I'm going to try to tell you now, if you listen and try to use it, you may just wind up with a publishable story here. Now your story here has got a kind of smoky reality to it, and as such I'm willing to give it more leeway than most in terms of verisimilitude or conventional methods. But even so, even with all that leeway, you've violated a few conventions which make it difficult for the reader to suspend disbelief. Even if the story is a piece of surrealism, in some way it has to fulfill Goethe's definition of a story as being something that might have happened but went unreported. If you think about it even Kafka's Metamorphosis or what's his name? Gabriel Marquez's 'Very Old Man with Enormous Wings' honor certain rules of reality and logic even as they suspend others. What you need to honor when you break big rules are the little ones. For example, how does the father in your story know the son's date and place of birth? How does he know about the scar on his chest? Worse, you depend on coincidence to facilitate the climactic scene of the piece—the father wanders drunk into the very alley where the son is waiting. In real life, events may occasionally turn on coincidence, but really only very rarely and anyway in a fiction we want more sense than we find in life..."

"Well, but the story's a dream," Serafino says.

"A dream."

"Yeah, you know, like Truman Capote's 'Tree of Night.'" He pronounces Capote in two syllables. "I signal that right at the beginning with the opening image where out the window the guy sees two moons and one sun. It's not real, right? It's a dream. Also with the title. 'Untitled.' Dreams don't get titles."

"But you called it 'A Passion in the Desert'—an interesting title by the way."

Serafino's face reddens. "Yeah," he says. "Real interesting. But that's not the real title. The real title is 'Untitled' cause it's a dream."

Twomey wants to get through the testiness here, to see what's there. "'A Tree of Night' had a title."

"Well, yeah, but that's like another way of saying it's a dream, right? It's a metaphor. Like your story that you wrote called 'Night Door,' that was supposed to be a dream, too, right?"

"You read that?"

"I read every word of yours I could get my hands on."

"Yeah but that story was in like the tiniest journal imaginable."

"Still. I like to know what my teachers have published."

"Well I am impressed, and okay I can almost buy what you say about the story being a dream, I can almost suspend disbelief on that account, but then you wrap it all up so neatly at the end with the police arresting him for necrophilia and all. And you end it very formally, with a repetition of the opening image. If it's a dream, you're not talking about crime and punishment or..."

"In a dream begins responsibilities...," Serafino says, staring, and Twomey pauses, remembering suddenly that the tiny magazine where the story 'The Night Door' appeared had also invited him to write a page about how the story happened to be written which they published as an afterword, and in that page he had spoken about 'A Tree of Night' and dreams and the difference between stories and dreams and the further complications of those differences in the field of illusion, where you seek to create the illusion of a dream. Apparently Serafino is trying to score brownie points but has only skimmed the sources, has missed the point. And now he pitches another reference at him with the title, almost, of Delmore Schwartz's story about the guy trying to recreate and undo the moment of his own conception as though it answered anything. Suddenly what started with great promise begins to seem impenetrable, dense. Yet there is no denying the story is promising. The boy has talent. He glances at the student, is startled to see in the glance something he has not noticed before, a hard flinty edge to his face, an arrogance in his gaze. His chest appears suddenly deeper, broader, his forearms beneath pushed up sweater sleeves thick and hard, his hands large and menacing.

"Well, as you know, Mr. Serafino," he says, "I have to give you a grade on this piece so I'm going to give you an *omega*."

"*Omega?*"

"Yeah, the sign of resistance. It's a good piece which shows a lot of promise. If you want to try to rework it and submit it again I'd be delighted to take it as another assignment and you've got a very good chance at an A here."

"You think it's good, huh?"

"I think it shows definite promise. You have the right instincts, and that's important if you really want to be a writer."

"More than anything in the world. My father's a writer."

"Fiction?"

The boy nods as Twomey thinks about the name Serafino, and it is as though the boy reads his thoughts. "He has a different name from me, but you would know the name if I told you."

"Sounds like you don't intend to."

"I'd rather not. I have my reasons."

Twomey nods, thinks, Then why mention it in the first place? Asks instead, "How long have you been at it yourself?"

"Just since I started your course. This is my first story."

"Well it's a truly impressive start. How did you enjoy the NWP Conference?"

His cherubic face stiffens. "Not much. I felt really out of

place."

"Didn't your father ever..."

"My father never did shit for me."

The abrupt bitterness startles Twomey, who takes a breath, moves past it. "Well a few of your fellow students were there, too."

"Yeah. Like two girls who are getting it on, pardon me, with teachers. And Xavier Green who is like very weird."

"How so?"

He shrugs. "I don't care to talk about fellow students to teachers."

"Of course." Twomey is thinking about the two young women who he saw at Montpelier, wondering if it is true they are involved with teachers, wondering which ones. He thinks of Geoff Burns and Andrew Milton, feels disgust at the thought of abusing trust, says, "Please do be careful by the way when you make reference to teachers getting involved with students. It's a serious charge that could ruin a career."

"Well it's a serious offense, too, isn't it? To take advantage of a young woman without, without honor."

"Absolutely. I only mean that idle gossip can be very damaging. By which I do not mean to say you are engaging in idle gossip." He tries to lighten it up, grins. "On the other hand, gossip is a classic source of fiction so as fiction writers we would be cheating ourselves not to listen." He smiles, glances at his watch to signal the end of the conference. "Consider reworking that story, okay?"

Morning conferences behind him, Twomey leaves the campus on foot to clear his head with a walk. The air is icy, the sky blue and sunny, as he strolls through residential streets toward the shopping area. He thinks of Serafino's face, some quality it has that draws his eyes, something familiar even, as though he knew the boy in another life. Odd thought. Yet he is odd, too. That business about "The Night Door." But who isn't odd in some way? Who doesn't try to construct things like that? Serafino told him that Xavier Green was weird and there was a point they agreed on. Twomey had Green in conference immediately after Serafino, and there was definitely something unsettling about the guy. He didn't smile. His eyes stared. There wasn't a moment of easy interchange, no cues of understanding, no feedback. Which was exacerbated by the fact that his writing was very poor, a fact the young man clearly was not interested in knowing. It was difficult to determine what his story was about. It was clearly written under the influence of Raymond Carver, but trying to imitate the apparent surface flatness of Carver's prose without echoing any of the powerful nuances Carver evokes in the seemingly simplest conjunctions of phrase.

Twomey found himself considering strategy with the boy, what tack to take.

"Tell me a little bit about yourself," he said to try to change the pace, and Green's unswerving gaze met his. "Why? What's that got to do with anything?"

Twomey shrugged. "I'm trying to find out where you're coming from in your work so I can give you the best advice I'm capable of."

"Well where I'm coming from in my work is in my work not in my background, right? I mean I didn't go to any prep school or anything if that's what you want to know."

"I didn't either. I went to Bishop Loughlin Memorial High School in Brooklyn. *Loughlin fight for victory/Show your might for the right we adore!* It was the best of times, it was the worst of times. An all boy school and once a week, on Tuesdays, some girls were shipped in from the Diocesan girls' school for a dance. It was hell..." Twomey hoped the candor might loosen Green up but the lizardy eyes just kept staring.

The cold air in his nose, his lungs, helps. The heavy moments with Serafino and Green begin to lighten their hold on his thoughts. He strolls past brick stoops, windows reflecting sunlight, crosses the broad parking area behind the main shopping street. A rock group has their instruments set up in the center of the gravel lot. The guitarist tunes, shrill notes twisting from the big speakers. Abruptly, the drummer hammers a quick set and they begin to play. Chords, lead, three back-up singers and a woman up front singing a lyric Twomey does not recognize. He wonders why this group should happen to be playing just here, just now. A small crowd is scattered in a semi-circle around them. A blond woman, in her late thirties perhaps, catches Twomey's eye. My my. Sensuous type. Little grey in the blond but a nice smile. Her face has radiance. Blue eyes in the cold day. Slight smile of interest on her mouth. Why? What does she want? He stops to listen for a moment to the music and sees the woman moving toward him across the semi-circle. He is pleased and confused, intrigued, captured in these moments of precognition. Then she is standing before him. Their eyes meet and Twomey feels a shield lift away from his heart. He wants to sit somewhere with her, talk with her, tell her things, perhaps hold her hand.

She extends a piece of paper which he accepts and reads:

*OPEN YOUR HEART TO JESUS. TO JESUS YOU ARE SPECIAL. JESUS LOVES WHO YOU ARE. JESUS WOULD NOT USE YOU UP AND THROW YOU AWAY. HE IS WITH YOU UNTO THE END OF YOUR DAYS. OPEN YOUR HEART TO THE LAMB.*

In his heart, Twomey laughs at himself as he looks up from the flyer to see the woman move off around the circle. She glances back at him once. He winks and she looks away, unphased. Be a tart for Jesus. He cuts across to come up behind her, "One thing Jesus never did that is the most difficult thing a man has got to do," he says. She turns, flash of defiance in her eyes. "And what might that be?"

"Live with a woman," he says and winks again, moving off across the lot. He crumples the flyer and pitches it into a refuse basket. The paper ball bounces off the rim and drops into a half frozen brown puddle alongside. It occurs to him that Green is maybe weird enough to be the stalker. If there is a stalker.

He wonders which students were getting it on with which teachers or whether Serafino was talking through his hat. JoAnn Iacono? Sex gets in the way of everything. Who is after him? Serafino? Green? Why?

He checks his watch. Quarter past one. Knows where his feet are headed. To the cozy tables of the Railway Inn by the Long Island Railroad Station for a large glass of seadark wine.

## Chapter Eleven

Now it begins, Twomey thinks. He sits at the kitchen table, watching Jenny clean her tools at the sink, an assortment of knives and spatulas crusted with plaster. Nothing has yet been said but he can feel it is coming and senses it will be the end of peace between them. Nonsense, he thinks. Just panic. Still, he feels it. From the stereo in the living room he can hear the quiet formal sounds of the first movement of Coltrane's A Love Supreme.

Jenny says, "I spoke to your mother today."

"Did she call?"

"I called her. She's coming to dinner for Christmas."

Twomey is fiddling with the sugar bowl, thinking about a taped interview he once saw with Coltrane in which he or the interviewer spoke about music as the key to the vibrations that hold matter intact. He digs the spoon into the sugar, slowly turns it so that sugar spills back into the bowl. "How did you manage that?"

"I just called her, Freddy. I just asked her again. That's all it took. She just needed to know you really wanted her to come, Freddy." She glances at him. "If you did."

"Now what is that supposed to mean?" He notices that when she calls him "Freddy" at the end of each sentence, it is meant as an ironic intimacy and almost takes out his pocket pad to write it down. "Of course, I wanted her to come. I asked her, didn't I? She is not always lucid, Jenny. You just got her at a better moment than I did." Even as he says this he realizes some part of him hoped to be free of her. "It's a no-win situation, Jen. It's a drag if she comes, it's a drag if she doesn't." Coltrane's plaintive sax is calling parallel question sounds in the next room and he wishes he could retreat, wrap himself in the

133

darkness and the sound.

"I feel there are things that you and I don't really know," she says, this time without a glance, and Twomey realizes that he has played right into whatever it is that he feared was about to happen. That it was that much closer to happening now. "Okay, now maybe this will sound brutal, but doesn't a man have a right to enjoy Christmas with his wife and children without being plagued by a senile relative."

"Your mother, Freddy," she says, and Twomey feels a smile almost break on his face; the way she said it made him think of one Puerto Rican saying to another, "Tu madre." She repeats it. "Your mother, Freddy. Not a relative. Your mother."

"You're a clannish lot, you mothers."

"This is not funny, Freddy."

"I know it's not funny, but nothing is just serious either. I did say it would sound brutal, didn't I? I'm trying to be honest about my feelings. I don't like feeling that way, but that's how I feel. Sometimes we have feelings we don't want to have."

She wipes a brush, lays it on the drainer, looks at him. "This debate you're having with yourself surprises me. It's the kind of question a man of your age ought to be able to settle inside yourself and find the decent solution."

"Decent."

"Yes."

Some part of him, the writer part, is intrigued by this exchange. How fortunate she is, he thinks, to be able to believe in a single dominant fibre of character. Decency. He says, "I think tactile artists have a less complex relationship with reality than those who work with words."

This time her glance is decidedly not a friendly one. "Something you said once, years ago. It seemed funny at the time, but it always bothered me. Now I'm beginning to understand why."

Here we go. "I have a feeling you intend to say more."

"You told a story. It was at a party. I don't remember what. But we were telling about something that happened to us and you turned the facts all around. You changed things around. Finally, I couldn't hold my tongue, I said, Freddy, that's not how it happened at all, and you said, No, but what really happened would make such a lousy story, and everybody laughed. I laughed, too. I was charmed by the wicked openness. But it's not funny anymore."

"I can't believe this." Twomey rises, paces to the window, looks out at the dark night, the snowy yard, opens the refrigerator, looks in, shuts it again. "I can't believe that you truly believe that things can be otherwise. And you misquoted me by the way. I believe what I said was something like, If I told what really happened it wouldn't be as true."

"I'm not really criticizing you, Freddy. But I do hope you know the difference."

"The difference?"

"Between what is real and what is not."

"Oh, come on, Janet!"

"Who?"

"What?"

"What did you call me?"

"Jenny."

"You called me Janet."

"Why would I do that?"

"I don't know. Why would you? Why would you blush? Do you know anyone named Janet?"

He plunges on quickly. "Jenny, if you insist that the only truth is in the raw undigested linear facts of experience you are dooming yourself to drown in information. And any moment anyway has more than a linear surface—it has depth, breadth, height and time, and time has past present future with depth, breadth, height. Christ, you're an artist—what's cubism tell us if not that if you try to see a thing from every angle, it becomes hopelessly distorted. It's another view of reality. Newman's Voices. Remember that one? A blank white canvas with three tiny black specks on it. Everything. And nothing. Pollock. The overwhelming all. Every goddamn thing that is told is a selection and rearrangement, and it is all a point of view. Klee said that. 'Reality is but a point of view.' When you read the New York Times you are reading fiction of a sort. The stories told by witnesses in the court of law are fictions which are then interpreted by jurors under the influence of literary critics with law degrees. We're all looking at life and we each see it from our own point of view and maybe they're damn close sometimes, most of the times, but it is never exactly. What we see is imperfect and we try to make sense of it. You don't make sense of a wall by describing every goddamn pattern in every goddamn brick that makes it up for Christ's sake! The, the FBI even, I read in the papers the other day that the FBI when they're investigating a case, they look first for physical evidence. Witnesses are secondary because their perceptions are untrustworthy."

She gathers her tools in one hand and lays them carefully into a metal box which she shuts and latches.     Her eyes, green and cool, meet his. Quietly, she asks, "Did you ever have another woman while we were married?"

The moment of decision is interminable. He lives it as a game of chess he did not even know he was playing and which he fears might lose him everything. Check to the left, checkmate to the right. He must answer or be judged by his silence. There seems no other way. He hears his voice say, "No, I have not. And I told you that before. Do I need to tell you everyday?"

Her face is calm, her eyes knowing. He sits again, trying to divine the dimensions of the trap in which he finds himself. He feels his own perimeters have been violated, that he has been staked on a spit of simplisms and sentenced to be roasted alive for the crime of having developed a knowledge of his own complexity, the complexity of human comprehension with which he has worked as a writer for the bulk of his adult years. How to begin to present the core of your being to someone who was looking for an excuse to deny its validity? But somewhere amidst that is another fear. The fear that she already knows about Janet. That Geoff has told her. That she is biding her time to see how long it will take before he tells her. How many times she will have to give him the opportunity to tell before he takes it and stops lying.

"No," she says finally. "It's all right. You don't have to do that, but..."

Twomey lifts his face to see Jimbo standing in the kitchen doorway, looking from the one to the other of them. How long had he been there?

"This is a private discussion," Twomey snaps at him, and the boy's lip curls with disdain. "I can see that," he says and turns from the room. Twomey hears the boy's steps on the staircase up to his room. He remembers his uneasiness about Jimbo, whether the boy could somehow have done this. He could have slipped the shorts into his bag when he got home. Twomey tries to remember whether there was an opportunity. He looks at Jenny who stands over the sink now, water running on the back of her wrist. He is tempted to mention Jimbo to her, but he can not. He remembers the feel of the bottoms of Janet's feet against his palms. The rough callus. What a mistake it was to go with her, he thinks. And her name slipping out of his mouth without his even knowing it. As though begging to be discovered. But really nothing happened, he had not really lied. And if he opted for the truth it could only be part truth anyway because he could not tell about Catherine those years ago. How many now? Five, six? That had gone on for weeks. That had been substantial. But now it was long behind him. He puts it from his thoughts, returns it to a past that is dead and gone and of which he is safely free. He remembers now having seen her at the Plaza. Could it have been her? Nonsense! How? He remembers Geoff Burns at Julio's, his unashamed attempt to philander. Janet's unashamed will to be involved with him. Do people just live with that? How?

He wants to say something to Jenny but fears upsetting her. This precarious balance they have achieved, even unsatisfactory as it is, is better than more questions, better than the need to repeat his lie again.

"Jenny," he whispers. "Someone is trying to ruin me. I need you to be here for me. I need you to believe in me."

Her eyes meet his. "I'll be here for you."

He takes the car, despite his horror of winter driving. His back is chill with sweat as he steers around a long curve through the woods, headed east on the north shore, alert to the feel of the road, wondering if he is trying to play Russian roulette with the vehicle. That would be one solution. Do like your brother did. The end.

The woods are lovely in the snow, like Frost's "Snowy Woods," a poem Jimbo always loved from when he was just a tiny kid. Twomey used to do poetry play with them, using the Kenneth Koch books on writing poetry with children, and he can still remember the breakthrough day when Jimbo suddenly graduated from stiff moralistic word salads to one that was truly a poem, about a cat in the snow, trying to enter a basement.

Where is the Jimbo of yesteryear?

Jimbo, are you doing this to me, son? Have I somehow hurt you so badly? And *how*?

He is through the woods now, headed past a strip of motels toward the next town. A light snow begins to fall. He parks the car on a side street and enters the town on foot. West Egg, he thinks. The eyes of the strange doctor upon me. Poor Fitzgerald. Poor Zelda. For all their success, doomed lives. Then he sees himself feeling sorry for F. Scott Fitzgerald and snorts, shivers to shake free of sentiment and self-pity. He remembers a friend of his, a tough guy, ex-Marine, highly decorated noncom from Vietnam, whose wife was leaving him and Twomey asked how he was holding up, and the guy said, "This is the toughest one I ever had to face. I figure, I'm supposed to be tough. Let's see if I am."

Let's see if *I* am.

Twomey crosses a street into the commercial area, street draped across with wired fir branches, plastic decorations, a shop window with an automated laughing Santa, hammering elves. He remembers for some reason a toy truck he got for Christmas as a kid, a metal dump truck the size of an egg carton, and in the back of the truck was a box of lead cowboys and Indians, each tied individually with string on a cardboard backing. What treasures they seemed. He can still recall sitting on the floor in front of the tree playing with the things, his brother Jimbo nearby playing with *his* presents, his father drinking eggnog at the table, mother in the kitchen, and the aroma of turkey stuffing in the air. A family.

He feels the snow gathering in his hair, the chill through his black dungarees, the thin leather soles of his shoes. He digs his fists deeper into the side pockets of his leather jacket and knows suddenly where he is going.

Miraculously, the side door of St. Sebastian's is open. The interior is dim and empty as the heavy door hinges slowly shut with a squeak behind him. With one glove he dusts snowflakes off his shoulders, pats his hair dry with his handkerchief. He dips his fingers into the holy water font, blesses himself, steps up the side aisle, genuflects and kneels in the first pew. Between the side and center altar is a statue of St. Sebastian stuck with arrows. Twomey tries to recall the legend, something about him curing the populace of some disease borne by arrows? Couldn't be right.

He considers himself kneeling there, an apostate, recognizing the church for what it is, as a system of lies used to control the people, dirty-hearted priests molesting children, but still feels cheated of the comfort of those lies. He still cherishes the New Testament and can find comfort from it, but it was not the same as having the church itself.

Well, here you are, Twomey. You have gone to the altar of God, God the joy of your youth. What now? What do you do? Put on a Jimmy Stewart mask and mutter, *Lord, I'm not a praying man...?*

The familiar stone smell of the church, the light of snow and street lamps through the stained glass windows casting patches of color across the altar, the smell of candles, the comforting hardness of the kneeler, the intense familiarity of the place coupled with its alienness, all combine, converging in Twomey's chest in a sensation of tightening, a hard tight ball. He recognizes the sensation as a prelude to tears, turns his face up to the stained glass light to help induce them. His eyes burn, the surface of his skin tingles with gratitude for the impending release. How long since he last wept? Decades. Oh please let me now, yes. But he feels himself locked in the instant just before the release of weeping and nothing happens; and he feels it is his own fault and does not know why.

This sense of himself kneeling there, responsible for his own unworthiness, ignorant of the cause of his guilt, disinclined to begin a process of self-accusation—blame is everywhere, in every act, you cannot help that you are alive, human, weak, susceptible, that you feed your life with the life of other creatures, these are the conditions

139

of an existence into which we stumble alone and ignorant. But are we required to require more of ourselves? To rise above these brutal conditions? To become greater than them, even if that greatness is only slight, tenuous, yet still delivers us to a moment of...what? Love? Perfect love? A true sense of love stronger than the ego? Love Supreme?

Love.

The word seems for a moment the answer to a question that for years has bedevilled his existence, but at the same moment turns before his writer's eye to elicit judgement—cliché!—and so judged eludes him. The sense of hope that had surprised him floods away and once again he is left alone with himself, his own paltry existence, the arid place in his heart where tears should be.

One wall of the church is lined with windows depicting a series of Old Testament motifs and Twomey thinks of the songs of Jeremiah (Why doth mine enemies prosper even as they afflict me o lord!) which so often have given him comfort even as he viewed with some amusement their almost Nixonesque plaint and plea for deliverance from enemies.

His amusement gives way to a sense of himself surrounded by unknown enemies who are after him for reasons he does not understand. People he always considered friends, colleagues, benevolent companions of his life—Burns, his students, a woman he almost slept with, even his children—now seem prepared to destroy him.

The emotion in his chest breaks. He hears his own sob echo in the church and as a single tear burns out of his eye, he hears his own loud whisper: "Why?" And again, like the croak of a sick frog, "Why?"

A few tears roll down his cheeks, nothing more, yet he feels a certain release, feels he has been close to an understanding he wants to embrace. *Love*? Like in the sixties? *All you need is...* The thought of the sixties troubles him, like the memory of a latent toothache.

A rustling from behind startles him. He hears the church door hinge shut with a loud squeak. He rises quickly, turns, scans the aisle, the pews, hears the muted thump of his own feet hurrying to the vestibule. There is no one, nothing. He opens the front door, hears again the squeak of the hinge, as the door thumps shut behind him.

It is still snowing. The street before the church is empty yet there are footsteps leading from the door. Someone was there. Someone heard him sob, heard his plaintive why, and left again. Who wouldn't leave? Take you for a mental case.

He digs his clenched fists into his jacket and walks slowly back to his car in the falling snow, thinking morosely of Jenny at home with her very quiet anger. If only he could just buy a bottle of wine, say, Hey, Jen, let's put on some romantic soul music and dance a little, sit by the front window by candlelight and hold hands, kiss... *Sweeter than the fruit/Of the cherry so sweet/I'm so proud/So proud of you...*

Halfway to his car he stops, feeling on his forehead the tickle of an absence—he has failed to dip his fingers in the holy water font on his way out of the church, failed to bless himself. Force of ritual, of broken ritual. He rubs his forehead with the tips of his fingers to soothe the absence.

His car sits in a circle of copper light from a tall chrome street-lamp. It is covered completely with a thin layer of snow, windows and all, and he thinks how quiet and cozy it would be to just sit inside there, closed in by the snow. There are some marks on the windshield which, as he gets closer, he sees are words printed in the snow. Block letters that say, *CUZ YOU A PRICK.*

The road is iced with snow. Towmey's foot barely touches the gas as he steers back through the woods. Lovely, dark, and deep. And he is thinking of a student he had a few years ago, Charles Porter, a black kid who was writing a series of poems he called Dog Heads Each poem was about a different kind of dog that he likened to a human being. Twomey encouraged the work, but young Porter was insatiable for encouragement. He began showing up more and more frequently at Twomey's office, every day, twice a day sometimes, with poems under his arms, or sometimes just to talk. He wanted Twomey's advice about everything—whether he should take trumpet lessons, how he should deal with his father, his girlfriend, whether he should sleep with her, whether he should take a leave of absence from school and join the Navy. He told Twomey he had never made love with a woman and wondered if there was something wrong with him. He got hold of

Twomey's home number and phoned him there one evening. Twomey felt for the kid, gently suggested he talk with his priest or a "counselor," but finally he had to distance him, draw back, cut the meetings short, keep it focused on the poetry which, truth told, was good but not great. Then suddenly he never saw Charles Porter again. Perhaps he'd found another teacher to latch on to. Perhaps he'd joined the Navy. Twomey pictured the boy in Navy whites walking the streets of Barcelona, say, looking for a whore. Then he saw Porter's picture in the papers, on the obit page. He was being waked at a funeral home in Jamaica. The article said he had died cleaning his hunting rifle, was survived by two sisters, his mother and his father who was a policeman.

Twomey drove down to the wake, stood uncertainly in the door of the chapel, but almost at once a young black girl hurried to him. She put her arms around him and said with such feeling Twomey felt water in his eyes, "Oh Mr. Twomey, Charles would have been so happy you came. You were his god."

This was Earline, the girlfriend. She introduced him to the two sisters, both beautiful, both models, and the father who Twomey recognized at once as one of the Dog Heads—a bulldog. "You that, uh, *poetry* teacher," the man said. "You tell my boy he should see a, uh, counselor?"

Why do I think of that now? Twomey asks himself as he eases up on the pedal approaching an overpass. Could be ice there in the dark beneath that bridge. How does Charles Porter fit into my thoughts? The feeling of guilt? Why guilt now? This is not my doing? What then?

The diction. It's black diction. *Cuz you a prick*. Is it a black kid then? Or is that just a smokescreen? Or is there some double meaning there? *Cuz* as because and cuz as a verb—cause you to have a prick—a stab or a cut. If it was just meant as mind-fucking, it is working.

In his rearview the lights of a car behind him sting his eyes. Brights. It falls back. Twomey recognizes the snout of an old Chevy. It hangs there on his tail, and he thinks maybe that's him, maybe this is it. The possibility gives some sense of relief. A confrontation finally. He slows even more, steers into the shoulder of the road and brakes carefully, thinks, *Okay, here I am, what's the game?*

But the driver behind him guns the engine, and the Chevy swerves impatiently around him and lurches past.

Nothing.

## Shadow King

You watched him from the shadows of the church and all you could think was You dumb mother fucker you are so easy. It was amusing in a way to see him hunched over the back of the pew there, stripped naked you might say. All his theories and cocksure manner gone. He was weak, soft. Wouldn't last two days some of the places you been. He was under and it was your power that did it to him. Now you had him.

Then you remembered that he was yourself in a sense. You were him. What he did to you deserved pay back and here you were. The fucking word made flesh.

The fourth notebook is almost full. Blow on your fingers, chilled still from the cold, bare fingers on the wheel of the Chevy. Write, *Double hex on double-em is you know who*. Write, *The man is a sham*.

Write, *Message from the edge*. Write, *Whack time, daddy*. Consider that phrase, think what it would do to him. *Whack for my daddy-o*! See it, as if in a dream, him finding those words, sees his hand shake holding the paper. So scared. Face so soft with fear.

*What time is it daddy? Whack time. Whack for my daddyo!*

Across the room Laura is moving quietly, doing the things you have directed her to do. You stare through her, toward the window, and realize you do not really see anything. Something happens in you. Write:

*You never took me out*
*When I was little*
*so now let's say*
*it's time to pay*

*I take you out*
*Cuz now I am big*
*And You are little*
*Think about it*
*Let it fill the dull moments*
*of your days*
*Let it spill*
*into your haze and deep in quiet nights*
*O daddy do you not see*
*do you not ever wonder about me?*

Stare at the words, feeling a lightness suffuse your chest, your head. Power. Strands of power weaving together. The power of your own words combined with the power to create fear. Consider the ultimate power. To cancel a life. You would possess the soul of such a person as long as his life was in your hands. Is this a game? Are you really considering this?

Remember when you stabbed out Pardini's eye. Did it with a sliver of wood from shop. You did not feel good. That shaking in your bed. Disgust. But they never came back at night. No one wants an eye stuck out. You were safe and then you could forget.

It was the words in the book that brought you to safety. The secret master, Aleister. *Do what thou wilt shall be the whole of the law.* Trusting only myself. There has never been anyone you could depend on because of the current of malevolence started against you by him. The current that the secret master showed you must be reversed. First of all you must recognize that until you can depend on yourself, your own judgement, your own power, you never will have anyone to depend on. Your first act as a man was cancelling Pardini's eye. A magickal act, to take an eye, an ancient act. That opened the gateway to the path. Now comes the Night of the Walking.

But you do not know yet what you will do. Can you make him recognize? Is your power great enough to plant in him the seeds that will turn his evil back into his own sphere?

*Do as thou wilt shall be the whole of the law.* You have the power to kill him. You do. To take an eye, to take a life. At what cost to yourself? Carefully planned, carefully executed, none. Or you have the power to make him think you will kill him. The constant agony of terror. His knowledge that you are there, that you may be back at any time, that death is imminent, forever imminent. He would die every day then, every hour. What is the true way? What do you will?

You are so full of hesitation. Doubt. A bad sign.

And now at last, with the breath of the master at your ear, you see, finally: You do not know what you will do and not knowing is the true way forward.

Calm comes with this recognition, a lightness in your soul as never before, and you recognize further the presence of the secret chiefs and the closeness of *Nuctemeron*, the light issuing from darkness, and Goetia, the evil goddess, the ancient Sapphic crack, the Queen who knows and will not tell, she of the devouring tongue who must also be appeased.

Remember your dream then from the night before: You studied the straw matting outside the circle here in this room and three red ants crawled swiftly along the edge of the circle. You stepped on them, crushed them beneath your bare foot, but pushing down on the mats forced others to emerge, many large red ants and as you crushed them, pushing down on the matting, other large insects rose up through the straw, beetles, spiders, many-colored backs, many legs, hundreds, thousands of them racing across the matting toward the circle, and you woke in a sweat with a scream in your mouth: *God!*

And the knowledge that god is within you, not without. There is no god beyond man. The soul or center in man is the True Will and that is the only path to the limitless light. *To know. To dare. To will. To keep silence.*

Close your eyes again, slowly lift your fist to your forehead, a ritual of meditation taught you from the book.

This dream came to you on the wind, you search for the wind but if evil comes on the wind, it can only be undone by he who knows the wind, who knows to avoid the ancient unnatural ones, crooked, who hurt the eyes to look upon with their guardians of dog-faced demons sent by the Gods of Prey to chew on the bones of men.

You sigh, then, calm, satisfied that you now know that you do not know what you will do, that you must deliver yourself to this knowledge of non-knowledge by the ceremony of entrance to prepare for the Night of the Walking.

It will be simple then. You will meet him. Let it be on Christmas Eve. You will come to him as a star and give him the gift of fear and blindness and the acid of his own heart. Yes, Christmas Eve. That poem he always quotes. *Slouching toward Bethlehem. What great beast?* And, *A hard coming we had of it.* Oh, you have not yet even begun to know.

Glance up from the chair where you sit to where Laura works around the circle, cleaning the lamps of wax remains. She squats on her haunches, long straight black hair pushed to one side over her shoulder. She wears it down now, and her face is now clear of make-up. She tried to hide the pits beneath that paint. Pathetic.

*This is your face*, you told her, holding her head from behind, forcing her to look at herself in the mirror. *You had the disease when you were a child for a reason. It marked you for a reason. You hid it all these years until I came and then I recognized you. I would not have recognized you without the marks it left. And so I came to show you.*

Her face turned to you, her brown eyes raised to your blue-grey ones with the gentle trust of a child, kneeling between your knees.

Feel the power within you, behind you, building. The Secret Masters. The Angel. Maybe they really *do* exist. Maybe they *are* real.

The True Will.

You see now you had halfway thought it a con, something that you pretended to yourself in order to forge a frame through which to see the world. But now you see that imagining it, it becomes true. Maybe you are truly ascending. Laura scoops wax into the palm of her hand, balanced on her bare toes, squatting, knees together in tight black slacks and a blouse that shows her navel. Your slave. Your first slave. And your priestess.

"You will always be the first among them," you murmur to her.

She rises and crosses to the kitchenette, brushes her palms off over the garbage pail beneath the sink. Then she takes the box of beeswax candles and begins to place them in the lamps around the circle.

It should have been the fat of your enemy burning there, it should have been *his* fat, yellow fat cut from beneath his skin.

When the seventh lamp is filled, she sits on the floor on the outside edge of the circle in the posture you have shown her, one leg straight forward, the other bare foot on her thigh, leaning backwards on her palms. Observe her there, feel how your will stretches across the room into her. Think of the insects in your dream, all the colored backs racing across the matting as you tried to crush them beneath your bare feet. What were they but the slugs of weakness, of indecision, of doubt? She is watching you from beneath her eyebrows, eyes large and dark, staring. How easily she took to it, how it fills her.

She is your first. Tonight, before you leave to do what you must do, you will mark her. On the altar. Within the circle of flames. You will mark her, then on the altar you will come seed in her, on her, and will be ready to prepare for the final thing you must do to reach the Night of the Walking and reverse the evil current forever.

"You will always be the first among them. Always the first."

Her dark eyes stare. You know that you have found the way. There will be more followers to come. You will be freed of petty care. Free to tend greater matters. Which was destined always. From your conception.

## Chapter Twelve

Twomey is thinking about Bill Clinton, the stand he took, the persistence with which he refused to give in to the demand to reveal an irrelevant fact that was to be loaded with the weight of a truth that would topple everything. He stood alone against a legion of enemies, Twomey thinks. Everyone was against him, but he stayed on his feet and ended on his feet. He didn't let them destroy the world he had built, all the good things he had set in place.

He and Jenny sit in the living room, the night before the last day of classes before Christmas recess. A fine snow blows like white smoke in the darkness outside the front window. They are sipping cognac after a dinner of smoked salmon and steak, chardonnay and Beaujolais-villages, which Jenny would not allow him peace to eat.

She says nothing, poses no questions. She smiles, speaks civilly. But her eyes contain some unspoken knowledge. They seem to say, *I know you're lying but have to accept your denial, choose to accept it.* He feels exposed yet reminds himself that no doubt what he is seeing is a projection of his own ingrained Roman Catholic guilt.

He considers for a moment just coming clean. Open up the whole can of worms and dump it on the table. Be free of it. Unload it finally, forever. Be forgiven, or damned, but free. Start anew. But something tells him no, he must not, she does not really want to know this, it will not help. Now is the time to dig in, close your own mind to it, put it far away. Think of Bill, the Herculean Bill.

Nothing good can come of giving in now.

How he wishes they could go upstairs now and make love, put it all behind them. But he knows better. This will take time. Give it time.

Another brandy and Twomey stops by his workroom, stands in the doorway gazing in at the stacks of paper around his computer, the family pictures staring at him from their altar. Reflections of eyes captured on silverized paper by a trick of light played decades ago. An illusion that lets you see into the past, see into the eyes of people who no longer exist. He considers the eyes, staring at him. Uncle George with his dapper moustache and jug ears, dark eyes. Uncle Fred's light eyes, Aunt Viola's, his own father's, Jimbo's. What do the eyes say? What thoughts would they reflect if they could see him now, know him now? Would they be mindful of him as he is mindful of them? He looks again to Uncle Fred who left France at sixteen, must have had some dream of the new world in his heart. Was it worth it? And Jimbo who put the rifle to his head, blowing the music there to smithereens. The music of the dead carried away with the fragments of his skull, the slop of brain tissue spattered on the walls behind him.

He whispers, "What is wrong, Uncle Fred? Can you see me? Jimbo? What is happening?" Their eyes stare back mutely, unchanging, and he thinks of "The Temple of Eyes" he has discovered concealed beneath a flap of paper on the back of his own son Jimbo's closet door. A collage of eyes, cut out of magazines, prints, set up on a long sheet of pasteboard, not displayed but hidden behind the door. It occurs to him that that temple might somehow have been influenced by this one here, might even be a secret statement on it.

A movement in the dim light startles him. Nicola, the cat, stretched out on top of the radiator has raised her head to stare at him. He blinks to reassure her, but her eyes remain wide, staring. Yesterday, outside the bedroom door he found the butt end of a mouse which she had left there for him, tail and all. A tithe. A little tribute to the master. Or was it Cain's inedible offering to god?

"Why do you torture mice?" he asks her. She continues to stare mutely at him, yawns heartily, stares.

He carries his snifter out to the back stoop and leans against the doorjamb there in the white smoke, breathing the icy air. He fills his mouth with Hennessey and holds it there, relishes the chill air penetrating his shirt as he stares into the white smoke. Drink enough to recall dreams. One where he stands on a chair in his underpants at a party while some gay teacher tries to hit on him. It was supposed to be California and who was driving down some mountain road, a tight winding curve that narrowed with the corkscrew descent and who was driving? He closed his eyes in terror. There was a child in the back seat and yes she was driving, it was Katey, driving them out of the bright desert.

It occurs to him once again he has never told Jenny about Katey. It was so long ago. Before they even met. Still. Why didn't he tell? Shame? Regret? Because it put him in a bad light? Did it actually? Was it wrong, what he had done?

She was twenty-five years old. They lived in the desert outside Stockton, on a kind of commune. He was twenty-two. Sex and pot. Sex and acid. Games. Experiments. Magic. How they inched along the edge of madness. He thought she was the perfect match for all the desires he had suppressed all the years of his adolescence, a whole decade really of the loneliness of your room jerking off with desires, pictures in your head that seemed wrong, but not with Katey, they did as they pleased out in their desert kingdom, and life was such blessed stillness, a dream among dreams. The world a distant dream. For a time.

The long, slow distance between two waves.

Actually she was not well. In her mind. He could remember them naked in a room full of people as he leaned over her body explaining to her the great revelation in Karamazov. That all is permitted, and just then, at that moment, in a room full of naked people partaking of one another, he saw in her eyes how very unwell she was, and he knew he would leave her there in the desert, knew the distance they were to travel together had reached its end. But she had something to say to him: *Fred, I'm pregnant. I'm going to have your baby.*

In this life? Here? Where we live on dimes and quarters? Eat rice, when we can get it. No. There can be no children here. And of course: *My* baby? You're sure of that? Watching the hurt in her hurt eyes stare back at him. Again: How can you be so sure?

He got the name of an abortionist who would do it for what they could pay. It was one year prior to Rowe vs Wade. Right to life paradise. The time of the rusty coat-hanger. But they had a real doctor, an altruist, who would do it for what they could pay. But she would not. They argued for weeks, months, until he could see from her belly it was too late. There was nothing to do then.

So he got up very early one morning, and in the dim light of their cabin, he stuffed the few things he had into his knapsack. He didn't even look at her for fear that he would wake her, for fear that if she woke, his resolve would fail him. He tiptoed out into the pale morning light and crossed the expanse of sandy yellow earth to the road. He glanced back once at the house. All was still. Then he moved quickly to the highway.

Within minutes he had a ride. It was in a green '55 Plymouth driven by a guy named Al who was hungover and had been ordered out of the state of California by a judge who had been petitioned by his wife to keep him away from her. He was heading back to his mother's house in Indiana and offered to drive Twomey all the way to Indianapolis, over two thousand miles. The car door on Twomey's side was held shut by a screen door latch, and Al asked him, "So, what you runnin' from, son?"

"Me? Nothin'. I'm running *to* something."

"What's that?"

"Don't know. A real life."

Twomey has not thought about these things for many years, decades, has not allowed himself to, for Katey was so fragile, and he is not certain he can deal with it, the thought of her waking alone in the cabin, seven months gone, no money, hardly anything to eat there, and her mind not well. He remembers the hope he felt the day he met her in the library, then later on the beach cliffs in San Diego before they moved to the desert. Her long slender body, tan and blond in the sunlight, how her eyes shone as he recited poems to her. Donne and Thomas and Marvell. *I never met a man like you,* she whispered as he kissed her up against the cliffs. *You could talk the pants off of anyone. Tell me some more poetry.* Lips at her ear, "Yes, I said, yes, and my heart was beating like mad..." Not quite two years they were together. No longer than that. Almost a tenth of their lives at the time.

His brandy glass is nearly empty, and the cold is through to his bones, yet he wishes to remain out here in the white smoke, fearing if he goes in he will somehow be forced to confront the question of why he never told Jenny about Katey. What would Jenny ask him about it? *Did she have the baby?*

*I don't know.*

*You don't know? You don't know! How could you not know? Did you just walk away and never even ask about her, never try to help her?*

The familiar faces of the students in his workshop class suddenly seem foreign to him, his easy sense of who he is to them gone. Is JoAnne Iacono watching him now with interest or mockery? What lies behind Greene's slitted, lizardy eyes? Or Serafino's cherubic milk-fed beachboy face with its suddenly flinty gaze? Could it be something they all know about? Nonsense. Banish that thought.

Twomey sits behind his desk for a change, elbows up. He wants to dismiss them early, resists the urge simply because he so much wants to. But the class is nonresponsive, perhaps an echo of his own mood, and he is uncertain how to drive through the remaining forty minutes.

He is lecturing extemporaneously but the assertions he makes have an alien ring to them in his own ears. "What we're dealing with as fiction writers is, we're telling the story of what we can know. The moment we put the pen to the page we step out of reality and into fiction. Okay, so where's the line? If what we're writing is nonfiction we know that we do not have poetic license to rearrange, let's say, a temporal secession from fact as we may and do routinely do in writing fiction based more or less loosely upon real occurrences." He pauses, trying to call forth an example, but nothing comes forth. "But even the most objective writing," he says, "even journalism, must select and arrange facts in order to find a coherence that approximates the truth. Well, in fiction," he says and suddenly is uncertain where he is trying to lead. He stands, hoping the change in posture will jostle his direction free.

Joanne Iacono has had her finger up for some time; now she can

155

wait no longer. "Professor Twomey, I read something here in the textbook, I couldn't find the reference, but it was this woman who wrote..." She reads from her notebook. "'The evasion out of fear of some realities and the folly of that evasion because the realities catch up with you.'" Her big brown eyes seek his.

"What is your question, Ms. Iacono?" Hears the chill edge of his own voice, sees it register in her gaze.

"Well, I think it's true. Reality catches up with you whether you ignore it or not so isn't it something more than just like a subjective idea of reality?"

"Tees," he says.

"Huh?"

"T-i-e-s. Reali*ties*. The quote you read said reali*ties*. Of course there are facts, of course there are reali*ties*. Look..." On his feet, he gestures, repeating as if for effect the phrase which originally ran him into his dead-end, "In fiction..." He steps across the room, wonders what the students are thinking, what they see of what is happening to him, startled by JoAnne Iacono's attack—he realizes it only seems an attack to him in his state of mind. Is one of them here writing notes to him? Or is it Jimbo, his own boy? The possibility suddenly seems very real and it staggers him. He stands now gazing out the tall windows of the old classroom, his back to the class. *Never turn your back on them.* He goes to the blackboard, looks in the runner for chalk, opens the desk drawer. "No chalk..." He senses he is about to lose it for real, knows he should dismiss them before this happens, but does not know how to get from the moment where he finds himself now to a moment where he can casually wish them a merry Christmas.

"Look," he says then. "Here's your Christmas assignments. Find one true thing. Write one true thing, like..." What? He can think of nothing, no example. What? JoAnne Iacono's lovely mouth. You can't say that. Are you coming on to her? What is happening here? Snap out of it! He wants to run, get out, pictures himself fleeing to the hall, hiding in his office until they are gone, pictures their reaction left alone here, looking at one another, astonished, sniggering into their fingers. It occurs to him they might be amused, and that snaps him from it.

156

"So that's it," he says. "That's it for this year. Have a good holiday, and bring me back one true thing on a piece of paper—like..." He is at the door already, books under his arm, "...the mouth of your beloved..." pushing into the hall before any of them can buttonhole him, fleeing to his office.

He locks the door behind him, sits at his desk panting, his back and forehead muggy with sweat as he waits. There is a tap at the door. He sits very still, waits. Another tap and then, a moment later, the doorknob turns. One way, the other. Then nothing.

He sits there, staring at the date on his desk calendar. December 19th. He does not know where to go. At home Jenny's questions wait for him. Jimbo's shifting gaze and curling lip. The tree out in the cold on the terrace waiting to be set into the metal foot in the middle of the living room, decorated. Charade. Then he remembers he has promised Jenny he will drive out to get his mother tomorrow, bring her back for the holidays. He pictures her sitting beside him in the front seat of the car, poised and brittle.

On the stereo, to a background of gliding strings, Johnnie Mathis is singing that it's lovely weather for a sleigh ride together, as Twomey wipes the dust from a large cardboard carton on the table. Printed neatly on the side of the carton in thick black letters are the words *CHRISTMAS THINGS*. The words fascinate Twomey, seem to reverberate with a mix of warmth and terror, the known and the unknown, a new slouch toward Bethlehem, an army of "things." His youngest son, Larry, is standing by to help, clearly open to the Christmas spirit, while Twomey's mother sits across the room on the sofa watching them blankly, holding a glass of eggnog wrapped in a napkin on her knee. Sprawled in the armchair, Jimbo leafs through a Time magazine end-of-year special, an album of award-winning photos of recent years' events depicting various acts of violence and terror in Bosnia, Oklahoma, floods in Norway and Holland, an earthquake, the shooting down of an F17 by Bosnian Serbs, UN hostages chained to ammo depos, a shot down pilot who survived six days in the woods by eating ants. Twomey has read the magazine himself and wondered once again whether the unraveled knot of Yugoslavia was to become the start of World War III just as earlier it had sparked off the First World War, the place where Western Europe and, thus, the Western World, was bound together into a serviceable whole. Ironic end result of the velvet revolution.

He reaches for his cup of eggnog on the sideboard, raises it to Larry, grateful the boy is still willing to cooperate with the idea of Christmas.

"Cheers, Dad."

"Cheers, son. Mom. Jimbo."

Jimbo reaches for his cup without raising his eyes from the magazine; his "cheers" drips sarcasm. Twomey's mother stares at him with distant blue eyes. "Not really very much, I'm afraid," she says.

Twomey nudges Larry and points at the words on the carton. In a phony movie-narrator coming-attractions voice, he says, "The *things* that came to Christmas!"

Larry chuckles, does a similar voice: "A family. A tree. A box of *things*!"

Twomey laughs. He peels masking tape from the box flaps and begins to lift out the decorations for the tree which sits in a green plastic tank foot in the middle of the living room floor. It is a Scottish pine and cost a fortune which he blew in hopes it would help cheer Jenny up, but all she said was, "That ought to save our Christmas, I guess, huh?" Low voltage sarcasm, sting without disabling. It seems that is to be the tone for the holidays. No direct confrontation but she would keep him mindful of his sins by her eyes, her tone, the chill of her shoulder. Or was he imagining things. Projecting? *Hang on, Bill!*

He finds himself wondering whether this is in fact a matter of the unbridgeable difference between man and woman or whether there is, in fact, something wrong with him, thinks of a line by George Seferis: *The stranger and the enemy, we have seen him in the mirror.*

Brenda Lee comes on the stereo singing "Jingle Bell Rock," and Twomey takes another hit of his eggnog, eager for a good mood to bring him through this to the other side of Christmas. What might wait there he does not know, but can only trust it will include some manner of resolution.

Laid out across the table now are an array of ornaments wrapped in tissue and newspaper, things gathered over the nearly twenty years of his marriage, objects which the four of them are familiar with from this annual ritual of unpacking and hanging them on the tree for a few days, then taking them down, wrapping them in tissue again, packing them back into the carton marked *Christmas Things*. Even the carton itself is old, dating back a decade or more, and there are years-old scraps of newspaper in it used to wrap things. Twomey folds a little sewn toy soldier with cardboard rifle from a shred of paper on which he can see the face of Ronald Reagan just as Mahalia Jackson begins to sing, *Whose child is this/In manger born...*

"Don't you want to help, Jimbo?" Twomey asks against his better judgement, stung at once by the response, a cold, slow, immediate, "No."

His mother's eyes wander to a bowl of peanuts on the coffee table, stay there. She pokes a finger into her mouth and removes her bridgework, sets it on the table and places a single peanut on her tongue, begins loudly to suck on it. Twomey goes to the stereo, turns up the volume. Something, perhaps the smell of rum and nutmeg on his own breath, reminds him of the heavy woman who stopped him on Roosevelt Avenue earlier in the day. She reeked of beer and her own dirt as she leaned close to him, saying, "My husband's in jail and I'm pregnant. Would you give me something to buy some milk?"

Caught by surprise, Twomey fished a dollar from his pocket. She moved closer, trying to back him into a shop door where there would be no way past her. "Would you give me something more for some eggs?" her breath so close now that it penetrated the illusion. Whatever she got was for wine, beer, nothing else. He stepped around her. "Sorry," he muttered, "Good luck," and at once she was honing in on the next person coming as he turned up his mother's street.

On one of the top branches of the tree he hangs a little red glass Christmas tree. He remembers buying this, together with some other things, a delicate white swan, many years ago, before either of the boys was born. Where? He cannot recall. Macy's perhaps. So many details of life lost in the funnel of time. What was his life like before the boys were born? He can barely recall. Only that he thought he was happy.

159

All those years. He and Jenny. At the beach. Eating dinner together, watching TV, him writing while she worked on her assemblages, in bed, spring air at the open window, how he used to sing Little Richard to her, *Jenny Jenny Jenny, wont you come along with me...* Was it all self-deception? Did the past few weeks really change everything or had it all always been like this just beneath the surface, waiting to happen? These two boys who had taught him the love of fatherhood just a fleeting experience as they prepared to enter a world as uncozy as the world he had entered after high school. Those lost years of the sixties and seventies.

Anxiety touches him at the thought of his sons growing from him, the end of all those cozy years of their childhood that had seemed like forever, but gone now as everything goes, ends. My boys. Dad. *It's all so swift*, his own father told him once, not long before he died, and now finally in the echo of the years, Twomey hears it, thinking, *Yes, Dad, you were so right, it's all so swift.*

He glances at Jimbo there, demonstrating his apartness. Why? What has gone wrong? Remembers once he'd argued with the boys and words flew from his mouth, slipped out of him with no warning. *You snot nose ingrate!* he said to his own son and blushes now at the memory, that he would say such a thing to his own boy, that the boy would have those words to remember coming from his father's mouth. Let him be all right, please. Don't let him go off, crash somehow, ruin his life, please. He thinks of the little girl two houses down who the boys sometimes played with when they were kids. She is grown now, he saw her on the street this afternoon, seventeen years old and looks like a middle-aged woman, and Larry one night told that she is loose, drinks and carries on, was with four different boys in one night. *With them?* Twomey asked. *How?* Larry shrugged. Now Twomey's heart aches to think of her pain, confusion. He recalls her mother was an alcoholic, her father ran off. Life is so hard for young people.

He thinks of his own youth, involuntarily sees again the desert. His disappearing act. This afternoon again he went into Jimbo's room, looked in the closet and saw a sheet hung over the inside of the closet door, tacked down at each corner. He popped out two of the tacks and peeked under, to reconfirm what he had seen before, the door adorned with eyes: pictures of eyes in single and double, cut from newspapers, magazines, prints. Twomey recognized a Picasso eye, saw a tinplate of two eyes staring. Across the top of the door was stuck a sign that said, *The Temple of Eyes* and *Dig Yourself* and *Think this is weird? Catch an eyeful of the mirror.*

Twomey regrets having discovered this, beginning to feel there is no way out of the growing certainty that it is Jimbo who somehow has been stalking him and the growing possibility of this as fact so terrifies him he begins to doubt he can survive it. Jimbo. My boy. We were so close.

Immediately again he doubts it, hangs another ball on the tree, glances at the cat watching him from the easy chair. Eyes. Just eyes. Can I see just with my eyes anymore as the cat does? No words? He puzzles over why he is so fascinated with words, with putting things into words. Do I have to understand this? Can't I just enjoy it? Let it happen?

"Hey, Dad? Dad? Earth to Dad."

Twomey realizes he has been staring blankly at an ornament, realizes that Larry is speaking to him, smiling with amusement.

At that moment, from the sofa, Twomey's mother cries out suddenly, so sharply that even Jimbo looks up from his magazine. Twomey starts for her just as the telephone rings. He sees at once that there is not really anything wrong with his mother as she cups her jaw and whimpers, "I *bit* the peanut!" Twomey takes the phone, hears the tightening ball of frustration in his own voice as he says, "Yes, hello."

"I want to speak to my real father," a man's voice says.

Several seconds tick past before Twomey can find an angle of response. "Your real father? Who is your real father?" Even as he speaks these words, he senses he has set himself up, and the voice on the phone says coldly, "Figure it out, prick." The connection breaks. Larry is looking at him. "Who was it, Dad?"

"Some nonsense."

"I have such a headache," his mother says. "I've never had such a bad headache in my whole life."

"Jimbo, would you please get your grandmother a couple of

aspirins?"

Jimbo smirks, but complies, and Twomey studies his posture as he crosses the room, resentful and unloving. He looks again at his mother, her slack, empty face. Yet she does manage on her own. He considers this. How can it be that when she is alone she manages her daily needs? Could there be something willful in this? He studies her face, so old, so far from him, yet the face of the woman who was his mother, who had been so beautiful to him when he was a boy, who had cared for him, caressed him. How can I be so cold?

The phone rings again.

"Let me," Larry says, but Twomey cuts him off. "No, I'll take it."

"Merry Christmas, Dad," the same voice says.

"Same to you," Twomey replies. He is watching his mother as he grips the phone, listening, mind searching for a way to hold this person until he reveals himself.

"Are you having yourself a merry little Christmas?"

"Say, who is this?" Twomey asks mildly.

"I'm not surprised you don't know. You never cared shit about anything but yourself. I care more about the people I *kill* than you do about the people you're supposed to love."

Suddenly Twomey feels unreal. He turns his back to the room to try to keep this from the others. As Jimbo returns to the room with water and aspirins, Twomey realizes that it couldn't be him. Jimbo is here, and this voice on the phone is someone else. He speaks quietly into the mouthpiece, surprising himself. "Who *is* this? What do you want?" Unimaginative questions.

"I want to make you miserable. No, I want to make you know how miserable you already really are." The statement begins with a snarl but ends in a giggle, and the combination chills Twomey.

"Why?" he asks.

"You'd like to know, wouldn't you?"

"Yes."

"Examine your conscience. It's all right there for you to see if you will see it. But you're *blind*, man. *Blind*."

"I don't know who you are. I don't understand." He desperately wishes to get this in the other room, but fears the person will hang up. "Will you hold on a minute? Let me take this in the other room?" And, "Larry, hang up when I get the other phone, will you?"

"Sure thing, pops."

In his study, Twomey cradles the phone against his face. "Are you still there?"

"Sure thing, pops."

"Okay, Larry, I got it!" He hears the other extension click onto the cradle, regretting that he has spoken the name of his son so that this person has heard. Yet no doubt he already knows all their names, and more. The fact that this whole game has now suddenly escalated was a relief of sorts. It is all on the table now, almost, and more dangerous perhaps than he expected. *I care more about the people I kill...* Twomey's instinct is to put the phone down, shut the curtains, hide, but he realizes his only chance is to hang on, try to draw this person out.

"Look," he says. "Can't we talk about this? Let's meet somewhere and talk, face to face."

"Okay. That's a good idea. You know the restaurant on the north shore, off Northern Boulevard, called The Log Cabin? It's just past Bayside."

"I can find it. Shall we meet there? Give me a time."

"Great. Let's say we meet there tomorrow at six? That should give you plenty of time to fill the cops in." Something about the voice. Has he heard it before?

"I won't do that. You have my word."

The man laughs flatly. "Your word is worth shit. No. We'll meet all right, but I'll decide where and when. And listen to me: if you *do* call the pigs—and I will know so do not try to bullshit me because I am watching you—it will mean *severe* — you understand me—*severe* inconveniences for your so-called loved ones, you loveless prick."

"How do you know the phone isn't tapped? That I'm not already being watched by the police?"

"Because I know. I've been watching you. You're not."

"Don't be so sure."

"I'm sure. I know you. You're a squat and you haven't done a fucking thing to protect yourself or your family, which is right true to character. You got your head too far up your ass. So don't try to bullshit me, Professor."

The line goes dead.

In the living room, Twomey watches Larry clip the white glass swan to one of the short upper branches. The branch sags a bit with the weight so the swan sits angled downward, the eggshell white body almost luminescent against the green fir. Twomey thinks of all those years that have passed since he and Jenny bought the thing, a meaningless thing really except for the meaning they brought to it in the course of time. Births, deaths. James gone. Larry and Jimbo here now, two new persons for whom he is responsible.

He watches Larry's muscular hands trying delicately to straighten the swan on the branch, realizing it means something to him, too. And he looks at Jimbo, so grateful that his boy is not the one doing these things to him.

On the sofa, his mother's gnarled fingers rest on her forehead, her brow knitted and he glimpses behind the papery mask of her aged face the woman who was so beautiful to him as a child.

"Look at the tree, Mom," he says. "Jimbo, look."

One by one their hands clip and hang the little glass objects to the branches—a blue bugle, a paper drum, a red metal sled. The smell of stuffing wafts from the kitchen. He can smell onions frying, pictures Jenny stirring them into the bread fragments in the big pot along with bits of celery, chopped nuts, mushrooms, poultry seasoning shaken from a little tin. He pictures her face, the cold slack anger—or was he imagining, projecting, misinterpreting? He considers going out to tell her about the phone call, but if he tells he will have no possibility of pretending it didn't really happen, of avoiding the thought of it. Maybe it didn't happen, he thinks. Maybe this is a dream, a fantasy. Voices from the phonograph sing, *Let it snow let it snow let it snow* and Jimbo sits slouched in the chair with his magazine, and Twomey notes there is a scar on his mind, his heart, where James used to be so many Christmases ago, gone now, dead with all the unrecorded songs known only to Twomey who could not sing them. Twomey wonders if Jimbo will become a scar in his heart, too, if this estrangement will continue for the rest of their lives or if it is only a phase in the boy's development. We were so close. You were my first, Jimbo. I pushed you in the stroller for hours, long walks round the lake in spring, to see the trees in autumn. I used to whisper poems to you as we walked: *Loveliest of trees, the cherry now/Is hung with snow along the bough and Since to look at things in bloom/Fifty springs are little room/About the woodlands I will go/To see the cherry hung with snow...*

Your first Christmas, I trimmed the tree with you in the high-chair close by, watching as I hung many of these very things on the branches. He considers saying this aloud, wonders whether it would only annoy the boy, looks up to see his mother with the heels of her hands pressed to her temples, her eyes slit and mouth stretched into a wide grimace. Instead of sympathy he feels irritation. Her posture looks posed, stagey. She is still alive but already a scar in his heart, already gone, a casualty who has not lain down yet, although her picture stands with the pictures of the others he loved so fiercely as a child, his gallery of ancestors. *Forgive me, mother*, he thinks, remembering all the Christmases of his childhood, the same stuffing smell, his mother's recipe that Jenny uses, the turkey borne out on a tray, huge and brown while all praised it, the pure joy he and James shared, filled by the moment, never guessing the distance of their parent's hearts, their growing knowledge of the insubstantiality of it all, the slow remorseless drift of time.

How can I feel such distance from you, mother? What has happened to us, to me, to my heart?

As he watches her grip her skull, she says, "Mo," like a southerner asking for more, although he knows she means *no*.

"This is the worst headache I ever had," she says incredulously, and something in the sound of her voice alerts him, cuts through the callus of his heart. He puts down the glass ball in his hand, a large thin blue one adorned with silver speckles, as he begins to cross the room to her, and everything seems so slow even as it speeds up and regret foams up inside him.

"Mom," he says, "Mom," for he forgot to say certain things, to remember certain things, to give in to the tenderness of memory, to hold her hand and soothe her with words, memories of goodness,

"Mom," he is almost to her now as she slumps sideways on the sofa, her thin frail body writhing powerfully, head flailing from side to side, "Mom." From the corner of his eye, he glimpses Jenny coming out of the kitchen, sees she can feel it, and Larry stands beside the tree staring, and Jimbo, too, rises up erect in his chair, the sullenness fallen from his face. "Grandma," he says, for he too was once so close to the woman.

Christmas in the emergency room, then. They make it easy for him to decide, the man and woman in white—two doctors? A nurse and a doctor? They call him aside and explain clearly and quietly that her EEG is flat. Her brain is dead. They can keep her alive, but only her vegetative functions. (*Vegetable* is what they're saying.) The kindest thing to do, they say, is to turn off the resuscitator, but they need his approval to do so.

Twomey looks into their faces. A man perhaps a dozen years younger than himself, black hair cut so close the scalp shines through. And a fair-haired slender woman, pretty, with freckles, and a waist you could span with one hand.

"Is there no chance of her coming around again? Have a little more time?"

The woman's head shakes slowly, ruefully, and the man says, "Her brain is gone, Frederick. Her brain is dead." It annoys Twomey that the younger man presumes to use his first name. "All we are doing with this machine is forcing her lungs to take in air so that her heart pumps blood through her veins. It is artificial life. Nothing else is going on inside her. No sensation. No thought. No emotion."

They had mentioned their names but he cannot recall them, and they wear no name tags. It occurs to Twomey that probably the doctors and nurses who pull duty on Christmas Eve are the ones who have no family, no children. Or are they just the less powerful in the pecking order? Less skilled? Younger and less experienced? I am about to tell two people whose names I do not know to turn off my mother's life.

"I'm sorry," he says. "What are your names again?"

They glance at one another. The man says, "I'm Doctor Barth. I'm a neurologist. Ms. Heaney is the chief duty nurse in the emergency unit."

*Barth and Heaney*, he thinks. A postmodernist and a poet. Ha ha.

"Well," he says and hears the tremor in his own voice, "Well, Dr Barth and Ms Heaney, please feel free to call me Dr Twomey." Barth's eyes grow larger. "Are you a physician?"

"I'm a PhD. Now may I see my mother?"

The resuscitator obscures her mouth, and her face against the sheets is pale, the skin tight against the fragile skull, pale lids down over sightless eyes.

"Could she see?" he asks. "If her eyes were open, if she were awake, could she see?"

"Her brain is dead, Dr. Twomey," says Ms. Heaney, no sarcasm in her voice, and he feels a tiny tug of guilt at his outburst. "Even if the eye is capable of conveying an image, there is no brain to receive it. Like, like a camera with no film."

*Simile*, he thinks. *Never trusted similes. An overused, over-rated device.*

Her hands lay above the sheets on either side of her body, stringy and spotted, yellowish, like chicken claws. He thinks of a neighbor in the old house, years ago, named what? Name gone from me. *Marrot!* Once affixed chicken claws to sticks, tied strings to the tendons and gave them to his kids, Gregory and Clyde, and they went round with these sticks, holding them out at you, pulling the strings so the claws flexed in your face. Thrillingly awful.

The resuscitator produces the sounds of breathing, producing in Twomey a memory of scuba diving off the beach at South Hampton many happy summers ago, the regulator in his mouth, black rubber between his teeth, ears filled with the sound of his own breathing as he swam down toward the shadowy white floor of the sea. How many years ago? Twenty-five now at least. When Mom was in her fifties. How old she seemed then. Her husband gone already, but she still had two sons. Did she miss Dad? What is the nature of my mother's love for my father? What is the nature of human love? What are we

167

capable of sustaining in the realm of caring? The heart begins so full of tenderness, so full of sweet love, sustaining blow after blow until it goes numb finally to the boot.

Twomey's eyes fill with water as it occurs to him she is about to go where James went. A place. Or a noplace. Cessation of this. Beginning of something else. Or of nothing.

"Would you like a moment alone, Dr. Twomey?" the slender woman asks.

He nods—pictures her and Dr. Barth in some backroom with paper plates of turkey and cranberry sauce. He steps closer, his voice husky in his own ears. "I'm sorry, Mom. I'm so sorry. I wanted to be a better son. I don't know what happened to me." He pauses, watching her face. There is no change, no flicker. Her eyelids are still, her hands motionless. Only the resuscitator moves, like the inside of a vaccuum cleaner.

"Thank you, Mom," he whispers. "For...the beautiful years. The good ones when I was little, when there was so much love in the family despite everything, when we all cared so much about each other." He turns away but back again and lays his hand on her stringy yellowish one. It is warm at least, still fed with blood. "God bless you, Mom. I am sorry. I love you. I...hope you go to heaven. I mean, if there is one, I know you will because you were so good to us when we were kids, you were never mean," remembering with a jolt of anguish his fear as a boy of the death of either of his parents, of his brother, the dread of that desolation, and now they are all gone, he alone is the survivor, he alone contains the memories of their time together as a family, the only version of their reality is his, and no one to share it with.

Outside the room the two people in white wait and behind them Jenny and the boys.

To his sons, he says, "Do you want to go in and say goodbye to your grandmother?"

His eyes meet Jenny's. The boys go into the room, and Jenny follows. Then Twomey looks at the man and woman about whom he knows nothing but their names and occupations, and he nods.

168

As he steers the Toyota into the driveway he spots an old Chevy parked two houses up, an Impala. The fog lights are lit and a white exhaust plumes from the back pipe. Someone is sitting behind the wheel.

Twomey's hands are draped on the shoulders of his sons as Jenny unlocks the front door and they move into the house together.

He recognizes a truth in that moment, that despite troubles, despite whatever suspicion has colonized Jenny's heart now, mistrust and disbelief in him (or has he only imagined that?), despite Jimbo's adolescent disdain, this shared grief of death reconfirms that they are a family, that this family is his fate, just as he and his brother Jimbo and his sister had been his father and mother's fate. Truth in the cold dark air of a winter night, Christmas night, as the door closes out the dark behind them.

Inside, the lights are still burning, the radio still playing, *Hark now hear/The angels sing/A child is born today...*

Twomey squeezes his wife's shoulder from behind, whispers, "Want a drink?"

She turns, touches his cheek, shakes her head. "I'm ready to sleep. I'll just clean up in the kitchen."

"I need to sit for a while," he says. She looks into his eyes. "Don't be too long," she whispers. He smiles.

One by one the boys come to him. "Goodnight, Dad." Larry asks, "Are you making breakfast tomorrow, Dad?"

"You bet, Lar. It's Christmas morning. I always make breakfast on Christmas morning."

"French toast?" Jimbo asks, and Twomey's eyes meet his gratefully. His voice is husky with the answer. "You bet, Jimbo."

"Night, Dad."

"Night, Dad."

Alone in the living room he looks at the tree, almost done. Only two small boxes of decorations remain, blue and silver things that look something like segments of an orange. He goes to the front window and cranes to look down across the lawn to the street on the other side. The Chevy is gone.

When he has hung the last of the things on the tree and strung the lights through the branches, packed the empty boxes back into the carton and shoved that into the hall closet, he sits in the over-stuffed armchair opposite the sofa where his mother had sat just a few hours before clutching her head, flailing. Jenny leans in through the doorway. "Are you coming to bed?"

"I just want to sit for a while."

She nods, comes to him. He stands and holds her to him, feels no reserve at the core of her embrace, releases her and looks into her eyes. Is this just a truce, or are we past it? Has this death been serious enough to trivialize all that nonsense? She caresses his cheek.

Alone in the room he turns off the lamp, plugs in the tree lights and sits watching the tree, the sofa, the dark outside the front window.

He sees suddenly that for better or worse this *is* his life. He could never go from here. He could never be alone again. Not voluntarily. The other people he left in the course of his life are like shadows that haunt him, some pleasantly, some with twinges of regret or guilt. But these people here now, if he left them, would be open bleeding wounds for the rest of his days. There comes a point where you cannot do it again, cannot leave again. Too many people are gone or dead and he couldn't be alone again.

Yet he wonders again about that look in Jenny's eye. Whether it really was there? What did it mean? Would it always be there now? Doubt. On and on into the future. Or was he projecting it? It occurs to him in one blinding moment that he knows nothing about his wife, about her innermost thoughts. Then that moment slips away from him, and he no longer knows what he was thinking.

He touches the ring on his finger. Once, many years ago, he was at a picnic sponsored by his father's company. He was maybe twelve, thirteen. There were ballgames and hot dogs and hamburgers, corn on the cob, french fries, potato salad, foot races, refrigerated boxes filled with water afloat with ice and bottles of coke, Mission soda in every flavor, orange, cherry, rootbeer, and for the older people kegs of beer. The beer was served in a tent with no sides, and there was a juke box there, too, where you could play songs without even putting a coin in, just press the buttons. Toward the end of the day couples gathered there and danced. Twomey hung around the perimeters, spying on them. There was one couple in the middle of the floor dancing close and slow together to Jo Stafford's "Band of Gold."

*Don't want the world to have and hold*
*All I want is this*
*Just want a little band of gold*
*And seal it with a kiss...*

The sweet simple beauty of a man and woman with their arms around each other in the summer evening, in love, dancing, the music, the words, caused a sensation in Twomey's young stomach as if he was flying up in the sky toward a land of beauty.

It occurs to him now in his living room, watching his Christmas tree lit in the night, that he has reached that place. It is not as simple as it seemed then, but it is as beautiful, and he wouldn't trade it for anything.

A sound draws him from his reveries. He looks at his watch. Past three. Still dark. The room is chilled. He rises and goes to the front window, sees the Chevy there again. At the foyer closet he pulls on his fleece-lined jacket, checks his pocket to be sure he has his key, lets himself out the front door.

# Chapter Thirteen

The face of the Impala is broad in the smoky cold that swirls around it, and as he steps closer he sees that behind the wheel sits Serafino, a young boy with hard eyes. His smile is cold as he leans across to shove the door open. It swings out just as Twomey gets there. He hesitates, thinks, *Is this all part of it, too, what happens, the things waiting for me all these years? That one Christmas Eve my mother would die right before my eyes as I trimmed the tree, that I would come out to this car...*

Twomey slides into the front seat, drags the door shut after him, looks into Serafino's face. Despite the cold he is wearing a strapped tee shirt, dark blue, revealing his shoulders and biceps which are lean and chiselled, the wiry sculpted musculature of a gymnast. Twomey is suprised, impressed. He himself is in shape but is aware that he is older, slower, his muscles far less lithe. He wonders how he would do against the boy if it came to that. It occurs to him the boy is wearing the shirt to impress him. Maybe he can use that in some way.

The car heater is on full. Twomey unzips his jacket. "What's the point here, Serafino? What are you after?"

The boy smiles and switches on the headlights, clutches, puts the car in first. The stick is on the floor. Twomey cannot remember having seen an Impala with a stick on the floor. *Must be customized*, he thinks. He almost asks about it, then sees how ridiculous that would be.

"Where are you taking me?" he asks.

"You got so many questions when what I want from you are some answers."

The car swings left at the corner, heads for the highway.

"Answers to what?"

Serafino looks away from the wheel into Twomey's face. His voice sounds melodramatic to Twomey, an imitation of some movie actor. "You just don't *get* it, do you, Fred?"

"Get what?"

"You are definitely in denial, evasion. Don't you know reality catches up with you? That's what they been telling me all these years. Consequences. You do something wrong, they get you, lock you away. Maybe sometimes even if you don't do something wrong they get you. Like if you're a kid and your old lady dies and your old man is long gone."

He signals onto the highway. The three lanes are empty beneath the high lamposts and the cold dark-blue sky. A panel truck passes them on the right.

Twomey asks, "Are you my son?"

"And the blind shall see," Serafino says softly, and Twomey thinks he hears menace in the tone. "You've been much in my mind," Twomey says.

"How touching. And *you* have been *much* in mine. Very much."

"I mean not consciously, but somehow I think I knew, suspected all along that it was my...son, you, who was doing these things all along. Of course, I couldn't know if you were...a son...or..."

Serafino laughs flatly, and Twomey shuts up.

The boy takes the third exit, hooks right off the ramp and pulls into the first parking lot for the mall. Twomey glances at his watch. Not quite four. The lot is empty but for one or two cars —one with a tree lashed to the roof, another idling, white exhaust piping from the tail into the light of a lamp post. A few hundred yards away, the lights of an all-night doughnut shop shine onto the tarmac, no customers in sight. Krispy Kreme. Serafino parks close to the buildings—a pub called The Scott Inn, a hand-lettered sign on the door offering a Christmas special of mulled wine and eggnog; a cut-rate furniture shop; a news and candy convenience shop; a big revolving door to the heart of the mall, locked now, all of it closed and locked.

It's Christmas Day, Twomey thinks, Christmas morning. He

wants to finish this now and get home to his family, make breakfast for his boys and Jenny before she puts the turkey on. Half hour a pound in the oven, and Twomey can take a nap for an hour or two then get up and start making the *hors d'oeuvres,* stuffed celery, caviar on Ritz crackers. Then it occurs to him this kid here is family, too. A half brother to his boys. He tries to picture bringing them together, tries to absorb the fact that this is his son. He cannot feel it.

"So what was the ambulance all about last night?" Serafino asks.

"My mother died. Your...grandmother."

The boy's expression touches Twomey, a cross of pain and anger. "I'd like to say I'm sorry, but I didn't know her."

"Is Serafino your real name?"

"That's for me to know."

Twomey is trying to figure out where he can get to a coin phone, call a black cab to take him home, tries to remember if he has coins in his pocket, curses himself for his stubborn refusal to have a cell phone. He tries to think of this boy as his son but it all feels so far away. Like some technicality that counts for nothing. He feels nothing for the boy. Even if he really is his son. His and Katey's. What was her last name? Jay? Jayne.

"What happened to your mother? Did she marry?"

"You're not paying attention, old man. Like I said, she's dead. Long dead. She fuckin' killed herself. Pills."

"I'm sorry."

"I bet you are. She left a note. I was in a home but it got to me. It was a real nice story. She wanted me to know all about you. All about how happy you were when you found out she was knocked up with me. It made a real pretty story."

"You should write about it."

The boy laughs flatly.

"I mean it, you know you can really write," Twomey says. "You could be a writer. I could help you."

"That ridiculous story I gave you? And you ate it right up."

"It was better than you think. It was very talented."

The boy sits nodding. "So you really think you could make a

175

writer out of me."

"You are a writer. You just have to learn the craft. You could really be good."

"Like you, huh? Maybe I got a gene in me. Rich and famous. Must be at least a hundred people bought your books, huh?"

"There's a satisfaction to it beyond money or sales."

"Right." He is nodding, his smile almost merry. "Right."

He reaches beneath the seat for a brown paper bag. "Want a hit? Little X-mas cheer?" He removes a pint bottle, uncaps it, swigs. Twomey listens to the liquor slosh in the bottle. He looks at the label. Hennessey. Good taste. Serafino holds it out to him. He shakes his head.

"Suit yourself. This could take a while."

"*What* could?"

Serafino drinks again, recaps the bottle and puts it back under the seat. Twomey notices the kid is left-handed, remembers suddenly that Katey had been, too. The paper bag is still in his lap. He puts his left hand into it and draws it away with his right. The left is holding a pistol pointed up at Twomey's face. "*This*," he says. It is a large pistol of dark metal with brown wood butt plates. From the size of the bore, Twomey guesses it is a large caliber, a .45 maybe. Outside, a woman steps out of the idling car. Twomey is thinking he may die here. He fears being shot, pictures a large hot bullet tearing into his face, his chest. He fears the pain, fears this kid's power to make it happen, his power to keep Twomey dangling while he decides or waits for the impulse to move him, or not. He thinks about Jenny, about his boys at home, breakfast. He wonders about the rest, though, too, about death, whether he fears that. The insurance would take care of Jenny and the boys. And he would be free. He wonders if he truly believes that, if he truly would prefer not to be alive, if that preference has always been inside him.

"What's the point?" he asks.

"The point." Serafino smiles, eyes hard. "Count no man happy until he is laid in his grave. You taught me that, remember? Oedipus. That's a great play. I needed to learn that. Ironic that you should be the teacher, huh? Or that now I got to teach it back to you maybe.

To make you see. Maybe that's the point. Or maybe the point is that you should understand how you fucked me over and cheated me of what is rightfully mine. I get nothing. My mother got nothing. And those pampered assholes in your fat house get it all. And the only thing that comes my way is this current of hostility you set against me from the instant you knew my cells were there in her belly just trying to exist. You didn't know me. You didn't want to know me. You wanted me dead and that's not right, and maybe that's the point, and what am I gonna do about that now, huh?" With his thumb, he cocks the hammer of the pistol, and Twomey feels the rush of fear in his chest, on his scalp, the back of his neck. His eyes lift from the pistol, veer from Serafino's face, focus out the windshield where the woman stands beside the idling car, talking in the window, a pretty young woman in silver coat and sneakers carrying a silver shoulder bag. She steps past the side of the car. Twomey's eyes move back to the car she came from, see its taillights flick on as it backs out and turns in the opposite direction, humming away.

Serafino smiles and for a moment his face is sweet again. "Scared?" he asks.

Twomey nods, throat too dry for words.

"You think this is just us here, don't you? Just you and me? You see my face, my eyes looking upon you and you feel the power of the gaze, but you do not see the hand that holds my face, the hand of the goddess whose instrument I serve as. She is right here with us, Fred, Dad, Father, she is hidden in the background behind me like one of those kid puzzles you know, can you see the monkeys hiding in the tree, but you can't see Her. Ipsissimus. Her Very Self. You can't see her because *you* are bad news. You can't see shit."

"Are you going to kill me?" Twomey hears himself ask, and the question, the sound of his voice makes him feel pathetic.

"Well now I haven't decided yet, Fred. I haven't decided if I will or when I will or how I will, that is if I will, but I'll be sure to let you know when I do. I'll admit I *have* thought about it. I could see you there somewhere kneeling to pray in front of me while I point this iron in your face. Have you looked at it at all? It's a very masculine weapon, don't you think?" His thumb rests lightly on the cocked hammer. "As far as I could come now was to accept my ignorance of my knowledge of what I will do. To just sort of go with the flow of that, you know?" The thumb draws back and gently lays the hammer to rest in its slot. With his right hand he fingers into his pocket for a cigarette, presses in the dash lighter.

"I think I would have you pray the Our Father," he says, pauses to light the cigarette, puffing. "I think that would be appropriate. And you wouldn't know at what point in the prayer this lovely Smith & Wesson would spit in your face. I like that. But the thing is, it's like too easy, you know. *Deliver us from evil, bang!, goodbye, amen.* Nah. This calls for something more than that. This is a special occasion, and I want to use it to assure myself that you know about some of the experiences your first son has had during the life you abandoned him to. Hey, you know maybe it was like Oedipus in reverse, where you hear from the oracle your son will kill you, but in this story instead of sending the son away to be killed, you take off, figuring your absence will kill him or abandon him to the deadly elements, only to find out years later that your son shows up again and kills you for that very reason. Cause you abandoned him. That's a true irony, isn't it? Like you're always pushin' in class. 'True irony.'"

"That would make *you* Oedipus," Twomey says. "Oedipus winds up blinding himself."

"Shut the fuck up, scumbag, I'll fucking blind you. Maybe I will. Maybe that's an idea. Since I know you don't got the balls to poke out your own lamps, maybe I should poke 'em out for you. There are so many possibilities."

Twomey lowers his face, listens to the ragged edge of the boy's breathing, feels the trembling of his own limbs.

"That's right, old man. Do like you're told, and maybe I'll tell you a few stories about my hard times. Maybe I won't even kill you. Maybe I'll only, like, leave my mark on you. Kneecap you. Blow off one of your feet. That might be fitting."

"Do you want money?"

"Money. You think you can buy me off? If I want money, you'll be the first to know. Money. You shallow fuck."

"I was pretty young, you know, when I left your mother," Twomey

178

says. "Younger than you are now. And I had no idea she was pregnant."

Serafino peers at him, his lips parted over gleaming teeth. "Why you lying coward fuck, you *cunt*!" His right hand flicks out jabbing hard into Twomey's cheek with the lit end of the cigarette.

A second passes before he feels anything, then it is like glass, then pain, and Twomey yells, as much out of surprised fear as pain. He pulls back against the door, holding his face, sucking air through his teeth.

"You *knew* she was pregnant, you lying cocksucker. You tried to force her to get an abortion. You lying fucker, when she wouldn't agree to fucking *kill* me, you ran out and left her alone on the desert, and you *knew*, you scumbag, you *knew* she couldn't make it alone, you *knew* how weak her mind was, and if you didn't know what would happen to me, then you are too easy on yourself, *much* too fuckin easy on yourself."

Twomey closes his eyes and sees her face, sees her sleeping on the floor of the little adobe house that morning as he rose and carried his shoes outside.

"You know I watched you in class all this year and I listened to all your bullshit about what is real and what is fiction, and you don't know *dick* about life. You're nowhere near it, you pampered ass fucker, you make me sick, you make me want to puke in your face."

Twomey doesn't dare to look into the boy's eyes for fear of stoking the fire there, the boy's ascending rage, calling for more fuel.

"You *cunt*." He puts the pistol barrel against Twomey's nose, points it up his nostril. "Maybe I should impregnate you with lead." His thumb touches the hammer and the metal meshes silkily as it cocks and the eyes, his own son's eyes, stare into his. They are the same color as his, and he has the same nose, but the jawline makes him think of Katey.

"Some teacher. I could educate *you*. Ever been fucked in the ass? Huh? Have you?"

Twomey shakes his head.

"That's what they do to kids in the places I spent most of my kid years. A nigger come to me the very first night and says, *There will be*

179

*shit on my dick or blood on my razor, whiteboy.* But they didn't make no punk out of me. I learned how to protect myself. You don't know *dick.* When I was eleven years old I got tied down and butt fucked by seven guys one night, that's right, you think I'm lying, but it's what happened, that's what you left me to. But I tell you what, soon as I was untied, I got armed. They thought they made me a punk, but I had something ready for the first guy whose face I saw next day. Right into his eyeball, yeah, that's right, you think I'm shittin' you, tryin' a scare you, but I'm not. I put his lamp out for him. And that was enough."

Twomey whispers, "Jesus. Oh, Jesus. I was so young. I never dreamed..."

"To be that stupid is a crime and you got to pay for it." The boy draws back against the door and watches him. "What I am," he says then, "You did. And what I do, everything I ever did and everything I ever do, is on your fucking head in the *scheme* of things, as you're always saying to your class of numbnuts. From 'Paul's Case,' right? Willa Catheter. You taught us that. 'The scheme of things.' Well, in the fuckin' *scheme of things,* you gave me life and then tried to get my mother to kill me and when she wouldn't do that, you left me alone on the fucking desert with a woman who couldn't even take care of herself. You're guilty, man."

"I know."

"So what's the sentence gonna be?"

Twomey lowers his eyes. "Just to know is..." He doesn't finish, afraid it will sound like a plea.

The boy is chuckling. "Just to know, huh? Figure that's what you got coming, huh?" The boy's eyes watch him, speculating. Then, with slow care, he lays the pistol down on the seat between them. He smiles. "There," he says. "How's that for an offer? You take it, and you kill me. Just like in my story you liked so much. Come on. Take it. Come on." He holds his palm over it to stop the game for a moment. "But if you do, you better shoot, you better kill me. Cause if you don't, I'll jump you and get it back, and then you'll die slow." He removes his palm again. "So? Do it? Just think. I'll be dead and you'll be free of me forever. Just what you wanted in the first place all those years ago in the desert. I'll be dead here, and you can wipe the car down, and you're free. Who'll ever connect you to me?"

Twomey watches, considers. The boy is still smiling. He wonders if the gun is loaded. He wonders how fast he can move. He wonders if he could. Maybe he could just get the gun and shoot out the tires on the car, get away. But the kid would come back.

"No?" the boys says. "Not interested? You know what? It figures? Fits you to a fuckin T."

He takes the pistol from the seat, points it at Twomey's face again. "Too late. Anyway, they'd've got you. In my apartment is a piece of paper with your name and address on it and the whole story. They'd've got you and grilled you and put you away." The smile bores into Twomey's face. "Well, you know what, pops? I think I've made up my mind. I think I'm gonna let you go. I'm gonna give you a little X-mas present and let you go. How's that sound?"

Twomey says, "Depends what you mean by present."

The boy chuckles. "Figure it's a whatchacallit? Metaphor, huh? Well, no, it's really a gift. The gift of knowledge. You said once in class that for a writer it is always better to know. You said that, right?"

"I did say that."

"And you believe it, right?"

"I always did."

"Good. Cause I'm gonna give you a gift of knowledge about your sweet wife. She puts out."

Twomey's head draws back and he can feel the skeptical twist that leaps to his mouth. "Sorry. No way."

"No way? Oh, I must be mistaken. I could've sworn she's been fuckin' your friend, Professor Burns. Guess I'm wrong."

"She couldn't be so duplicitous."

"Duplicitous. Nice word. Well, I guess you couldn't be so duplicitous either, could you, huh? You and Janet baby? Tell you somethin' else to think about, maybe you should ask her, in fact—why's she visit your neighbor so often when you're not around? Know your neighbor there, the divorced guy with the red T-bird? When you were in Wichita giving a reading last October, she spent a good many hours with him. And you surely've heard the skinny on his tool. Word around town is the man's a horse."

Twomey shakes his head. "No."

"You really ought to plug into the grapevine, Professor."

"No."

"Yeah, I know, it's hard to accept right off. You just think about it for a while, let the information settle down in your head and get comfortable there."

Abruptly then, the smile falls away. "Open the door."

"What for?"

The eyes are flint now, the mouth small, the voice a whisper. "Just open the fuckin' door."

Twomey reaches for the handle. The air ploughs in across him in a wave of ice. Without taking his eyes from Twomey, the boy turns the key in the ignition; the engine wheezes, kicks over. "Now get out. Wait, roll down the window first."

The pistol barrel rests on the window jam after Twomey steps out of the car.

"Now stand there with your back to me and let me hear you start. Come on. *Our father who art in heaven...* Come on, pray, and start walking real slow and pray so I can hear you."

Behind his back, he hears the hammer cocking again and feels the urine spurt from him, down his pant leg. Twomey walks slowly from the car, his knees trembling, wondering at himself as he hears his voice reciting the words of a prayer he hasn't spoken in years, and each phrase seems the initiation of the last moment of his life. His back twitches at the thought of the pistol pointed at it, a blank spot where the bullet would hit. *"...on earth as it is in heaven...give us this day our daily bread...and forgive us our trespasses...as we forgive those... who trespass against us..."* He coughs, clears his throat. *"...and deliver us from evil...world without end...amen."*

"Now stop right there, stop walking."

He wonders if he could run, dive, roll over, but he is hardly sure his legs would spring. And a false move might just draw a bullet.

The boy's voice comes from behind him, a hoarse whisper he has to strain to hear, but he does strain, hungry to hear.

"Maybe I'll be back one day. Or maybe not. I'll have to think about it. I'm sure you'd be glad to see me, though, wouldn't you? Maybe you'd like that. You could invite me home to meet my brothers and your whore of a wife. Or maybe not. Maybe they're too good for me. I'm just the scum you shot out your dick into some cunt in the desert that you wanted some doctor to kill. You know what? Suddenly I feel like whacking you after all. You better go now before I get all pissed off again. *Go. Run*, you fucker or I'll burn you!"

Twomey's head is tilted to the side, listening, and he sees the flash from the pistol and snow flies up on the ground just in front and to the side of him as the sound of the shot cracks past his ear.

"*Run*, I said!"

Another flash, the bang, more snow, closer, and Twomey starts running, slipping on the snow as another shot breaks against the snowed-over gravel. He hears his own breath, his lungs sucking in the cold burning air and the sound of tires behind him as the Chevy pursues him. He turns sharp sideways, but the headlights, brights, turn with him, and another bullet slices the snow. He turns again and another cracks past his ear, he hears it as he falls, barks his knee on the gravel, slides, stumbling to get up.

The car spurts forward, circles him once, twice, swerving in the snow, and the face leans out the side window, the mouth open over words Twomey cannot hear. Then the car breaks out of its circle, lances across the lot to the roadway, shimmying as it peels out over the tarmac and disappears onto the highway.


Twomey walks home along the side of the dark road. His pants leg is torn, and his knee and the heels of his hands are cut from his fall on the gravel. He limps, following in the direction of traffic. The road is deserted. A car approaches from behind, and he steps off the road, waits in the shadows until he can see it is not the Chevy. It occurs to him the Chevy might have been stolen. He might already have ditched it, stolen another car. Maybe he would disappear forever.

Twomey's face is stinging. Gingerly he touches the burn alongside his mouth, winces, starts walking again. The cold air stings water from his eyes as he limps along the road. The crotch of his pants are still damp from where he wet himself. The wind gushes across him, and tears slide down his cheeks

From overhead he hears an eerie creaking sound in the sky, looks up to see three swans flying in formation, the white bodies phosphorescent in the grey dark of morning.


The house still sleeps. Just enough time for a shower and fresh clothes, and to turn on the tree before everyone starts waking. The living room curtains glow dully with the gloamy morning light. In the kitchen, he breaks half a dozen eggs into an orange mixing bowl, pours in milk, beats it with a fork. He carves out a lump of real butter and watches it melt in the skillet while he peels off slices of rough-cut bacon and lays them on the other pan. They begin to sizzle. In a few minutes, the aroma will permeate the house, wake the others, and one by one they'll drift down for a breakfast of French toast, bacon so crisp it crumbles between your teeth. Fresh pot of coffee. A jug of home-squeezed juice—oranges and grapefruits mixed. Their Christmas Day breakfast. They always have this for breakfast on Christmas Day. Then Jenny makes the stuffing, using Twomey's mother's recipe, stuffs the bird, lays long strips of bacon over it, and slides it into the oven while Twomey and the kids read the papers, watch TV, hear Christmas music, cozy, together. And when the bird is in the oven, Jenny will come out and join them, by which time Twomey would have made another pitcher of egg nog, heavy on the rum and nutmeg while the kids build a fire in the fireplace, and they would sit together with Christmas music on the stereo, Perry Como maybe, and they'd raise their cups of nog, look into one another's eyes as Perry Como sang,

*As long as you love me so.*
*Let it snow let it snow let it snow...*

He breaks another egg in the mixing bowl. It's light outside now, and he glances through the kitchen window just as Leo Zilka comes out his side door, broad-shouldered in a red lumberjack, carrying a bag of salt that he sprinkles up the frozen driveway in front of his shiny red T-bird.

Twomey turns his attention to whipping the eggs in the yellow bowl. The smell of bacon fills his nose with its succulent irrefutability as he hears footsteps overhead, Jenny rousing from sleep. He imagines her pulling on her bathrobe, tying the belt, pulling back the edge of the curtain to look out as she always does. And Zilka's big-nosed face turns from his work to look across at Twomey's house, up to the second floor. His thick lips spread in a smile that Twomey does not like, thick smile and slitted eyes that Twomey likes even less when it lingers on the man's mouth, trained upward toward Twomey's house, Twomey's bedroom.

For some reason he remembers a story he heard once about a woman who had killed her unfaithful husband not because he had been unfaithful, but because he had done so in *her* bed, in their bed. Twomey had never quite understood that before. He feels the sadness in his body, in his legs, his gut, feels it as weakness, a profound weakness.

The butter foaming in the skillet begins to bubble clear, and one by one Twomey lays slices of the batter-saturated bread into the sizzling pan, thinking about Jenny, about that day he met her on the beach at Hampton Bays, so long ago, and sang to her, *Jenny Jenny Jenny, won't you come along with me?*

# About the author

Alice Maud Guldbrandsen

**Thomas E. Kennedy**, a native of New York and American expatriate in Europe since the mid-1970s, is the author of eleven books of fiction, including two volumes in 2007—the novel, *A Passion in the Desert*, and story collection, *Cast Upon the Day*. Other recent novels are the four books of *The Copenhagen Quartet* (*Kerrigan's Copenhagen, A Love Story*, 2002; *Bluett's Blue Hours*, 2003; *Greene's Summer*, 2004; and *Danish Fall*, 2005), four independent novels about the loves and seasons of the Danish capital. A DVD documentary about the *Quartet* was produced by Harper College in 2004, and an essay about the DVD appears in *South Carolina Review* (Fall 2005). Kennedy's fiction has won numerous awards including the O. Henry, Pushcart, Gulf Coast, and European prizes, the Charles Angoff Award, and the Frank Expatriate Writers Award. In addition, he serves as Advisory Editor for *The Literary Review*, International Editor of *StoryQuarterly*, on the editorial board of several other journals, including *Absinthe, New European Writing* and as a Contributing Editor to the *Pushcart Prize* and is an Editor of the *Best New Writing Eric Hoffer Award* annual. He has also published four books of literary crticism, a book of essays on the craft of fiction, *Realism & Other Illusions* (2002) and with Walter Cummins co-authored a book of travel essays (*The Literary Traveler*, 2005). He is a core faculty member of Fairleigh Dickinson University's Master of Fine Arts in Writing program and has taught previously in the Vermont College MFA Program and elsewhere. Among other forthcoming work are a short story in *Glimmer Train* as well as various translations from the Danish. He is currently working on a translation of a book about the Danish physician, Inge Genefke, many times nominated for the Nobel Prize, who has spent the past thirty years of her life in a fight to abolish the use of torture—entitled *The Meeting with Evil*—as well as a nonfiction book about the bombing of the French school in Copenhagen, *Silence Was My Song* by Alice Maud Guldbrandsen. In 2007, the Association of Writers and Writing Programs (AWP) dedicated a panel at its annual conference to Kennedy's work, "A Lifetime in Literature."

For more information, see:
www.thomas-e-kennedy.com
www.thecopenhagenquartet.com

For more information on other titles available from
Wordcraft of Oregon, LLC
please visit our website at
www.wordcraftoforegon.com